# SECRETS

**Also by Bali Rai:**

*Trouble*

*Soccer Squad: Starting Eleven*
*Soccer Squad: Missing!*
*Soccer Squad: Stars!*
*Soccer Squad: Glory!*

**For older readers**

*(Un)arranged Marriage*
*The Crew*
*Rani and Sukh*
*The Whisper*
*The Last Taboo*
*The Angel Collector*
*City of Ghosts*
*Killing Honour*
*Fire City*

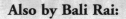

# SECRETS

## Two tales from Devana High

# BALI RAI

**Tamarind**

**SECRETS**

A TAMARIND BOOK 978 1 848 53119 2

Published in Great Britain by Tamarind Books,
an imprint of Random House Children's Publishers UK
A Random House Group Company

*Jit* first published in Great Britain in 2005 as *What's Up?* by Hodder Children's Books
*Suky* first published in Great Britain in 2006 as *Jugglin'* by Hodder Children's Books

Tamarind edition published 2013

1 3 5 7 9 10 8 6 4 2

The Random House Group Limited supports the Forest Stewardship Council® (FSC®), the
leading international forest-certification organisation. Our books carrying the FSC label are
printed on FSC®-certified paper. FSC is the only forest-certification scheme supported
by the leading environmental organisations, including Greenpeace. Our paper procurement
policy can be found at www.randomhouse.co.uk/environment.

MIX
Paper from
responsible sources
FSC® C016897

Set in Garamond Reg

Tamarind Books are published by Random House Children's Publishers UK,
61–63 Uxbridge Road, London W5 5SA

www.tamarindbooks.co.uk
www.randomhousechildrens.co.uk
www.randomhouse.co.uk

Addresses for companies within The Random House Group Limited can be found at:
www.randomhouse.co.uk/offices.htm

THE RANDOM HOUSE GROUP Limited Reg. No. 954009

A CIP catalogue record for this book is available from the British Library.

Printed and bound in Great Britain by CPI Group (UK) Ltd, Croydon, CR0 4YY

*To Class 7HO at Ripley St Thomas School in Lancaster for dreaming up Andy Stevenson; and to class 7L6 at Oakbank School (and Miss Angel) in Keighley for Matt Dwibble . . . nice one!*

| Northamptonshire LRE | |
|---|---|
| | |
| Askews & Holts | |
| | |
| | |

# CONTENTS

# JIT

# ONE

'You could have woken me up!' I shouted at my mum.

She looked up at me from the battered sofa in the living room and grunted something about getting back late.

'Lemme sleep,' she mumbled.

'But I ain't got no money for lunch,' I told her. Only she was already asleep.

I looked around for her purse and found it lying on the floor, next to a bottle of vodka and a load of other rubbish. It was eight-thirty and I was going to be late for school again. I grabbed a fiver and ran out of the house, hoping that I wouldn't miss the eight-forty bus. I was gonna get into trouble. Again.

The bus stop was packed with kids just as late as me, so I stopped feeling so bad. I wondered if my best mate, Dean, had walked over to our friend Grace's house, which is what we did most mornings. As the bus pulled up, I pushed past a load of Year Nines and paid my money.

'You wanna be careful,' said one of the older lads, Mandeep.

I looked at him and grinned. Yeah – like he was *really* scary.

'Or what?' I asked him.

'Just watch it,' he told me.

'Stick it,' I replied, heading upstairs to the back of the bus. Behind me, I heard him ask his mates what was up with me.

It took ages to get to school, and by the time I reached the main gates my head teacher, Mr Black, was waiting for me.

'What a surprise to see you turning up late again,' he said.

'Sorry, sir,' I replied, knowing that I was heading for a detention no matter what I said. No point making it harder on myself by being cheeky.

'I don't want to hear "sorry", Jit. I want to hear you saying "Good morning, Mr Black", preferably at around eight-thirty in the morning or at least by ten to nine,' he told me.

'But I was late because—'

Mr Black dismissed me with a wave of his hand.

'Save it, Jit. You'll need another excuse tomorrow.'

'Freak,' I mumbled, quietly.

'Detention with a capital "D" at lunch time, Mr Kooner. Firm but fair. Now get to your lesson before I forget that I'm in a good mood.'

I shrugged and walked into school, heading for my form room. When I got there, my form teacher, Mrs Dooher, was reading out a load of messages about stuff, most of which didn't interest me at all. The only bit I caught that meant anything was about football practice being cancelled this week. I nodded at Dean, who was sitting with Grace and Hannah, another friend, one of my oldest. Next to them were Suky and Imtiaz, the other members of our little gang.

'Miss!' shouted a lad called Marco. 'Jit is late again, miss!'

Mrs Dooher looked up and smiled at me.

'Yes, Marco,' she replied. 'I can see that.'

I glared at him. 'You'll get battered in a minute,' I said.

'MISS!' he squealed.

'Shut up – all of you,' Mrs Dooher said, not really shouting. She never did.

She was one of the few teachers at school who was OK. I liked her and I couldn't say that about many of the others.

'Late again, bro,' said Dean, as I sat down between him and Grace.

'Hi, Jit!' said Grace, smiling.

'All right,' I replied to both of them.

Hannah leaned across Dean and whispered to me, 'You get your haircut at that new place – BlindCuts?' she asked.

'You what?' I asked.

'Your hair, Jit,' she said.

I looked at Dean, who shrugged.

'Hate to say it, bro, but you got an Afro any black man would be proud of, you get me?'

I swore and stood up, heading for the toilets.

'Sit down, Jit,' said Mrs Dooher, only I ignored her. Not because I wanted to, though. Sometimes I get so wound up that I stop hearing what people say to me. My only thought was to get to the toilets and sort out my hair so that's what I did.

Dean came in after a few minutes, as I was straightening my hair with a wet hand.

'What'd you do that for?' he asked.

'What?' I asked.

'Just walk out like that? Mrs Dooher's cool, bro — she's always lookin' out for us and you just dissed her.'

I shrugged.

'Never meant it,' I said, feeling bad.

'You're funny sometimes, bro,' said Dean.

'Whatever . . . what we got first lesson?'

Dean let up and grinned.

'English . . . not that you're gonna get nothing done. You ain't even got a pen with you.'

'I got up late,' I told him. 'Forgot.'

'You best hope Herbert ain't got another snot-filled spot on his ugly face. You know how angry he gets when his face looks like pus pizza.'

Herbert was our English teacher and he hated us. Not that I cared. I hated him back, so I didn't care that he might get angry. He was nasty, anyway. He was always red in the face from shouting and that. And about twice a month he got these nasty boils on his face. During one lesson he had this proper beauty on his forehead. It was like another planet stuck to his head, full of pus. Halfway through the lesson he went to the toilet and squeezed it, only it started to bleed and he couldn't stop it. He came back into the lesson after five minutes and we were all messing about. When he tried to get us to calm down, we saw that the spot had gone and realized what he'd done. The whole class started laughing and he went mad. Dutty bwoi . . .

The English lesson was really boring and afterwards we had to stay indoors because it was raining. We hung out under the stairs that led to the Humanities area. There was me and Dean, Hannah and Grace. I didn't know where the other two, Imi and Suky, were, but that didn't matter. It was them that we were talking about. A few weeks earlier we'd caught them walking around hand in hand and found out that they were seeing each other. For a while it was like scandal central but I didn't care about it. It wasn't like it was any of my business anyway.

'. . . And they were snogging in the Science labs,' I heard Grace saying.

'So?' asked Dean.

'Ignore him,' said Hannah. 'He's just jealous 'cos he ain't got no girl.'

'Me have plenty girls!' he boasted. 'I had to get rid of my phone the other day. Thing was running red hot, you get me. Pure gal a call me on it!'

'Yeah – like in your dreams, stinky boy,' said Grace.

'You know it's true, Sister Gee,' replied Dean.

'I heard him get a few calls,' I added.

'Mostly from his mummy, tellin' him to come home for dinner,' grinned Hannah.

'Least my mum makes dinner,' countered Dean. 'You is so skinny I reckon you only eat celery or some other rabbit food.'

'Just 'cos you got an ass the size of London,' she replied.

Grace looked at me and shrugged before speaking.

'We're *supposed* to be gossiping about Imi and Suky,' she reminded us. 'Like, that's the *whole* point of being here . . .'

'I thought we was just hanging out,' I said.

'Yeah . . . we are. Hanging out and gossiping,' she added.

'You'll never make a girl,' Hannah told me.

'But why would I wanna be a girl?' I asked, wondering if she was going mad.

'It was a joke, Jit. You know, them things that are supposed to be funny?' she told me.

'Like Hannah's hairdo. That's an example of funny, you get me?' said Dean, making me grin.

'Oh, get lost!' said Hannah. 'Come on, Grace – let's go somewhere else . . .'

'But . . .' began Grace, only Hannah grabbed her by the arm and pulled her away.

'See you later,' Grace told me as she went.

'Cool,' I replied, hoping that I would.

I didn't want to go home after school, which was normal for me, and I was hoping Grace would invite me round to hers. Things were strange at home and my mum was on a bender again. She'd also taken back her old boyfriend, Micky, after kicking him out. I didn't like Micky and he didn't like me. He was a bully and the last time he'd moved in he started picking on me, calling me all kinds of names when Mum wasn't there, and locking me out. It got so bad that I had slept in the park for a night, until Dean's mum had spoken to my mum and sorted things out. The problem was that, with my mum, things were never sorted for long. Now he was back and making my life hell again. And that was something I could do without.

As I was thinking, Dean opened his bag and got out a load of copied PlayStation games.

'Come, Jit – we got money to make,' he told me, handing me the copies.

We sold all kinds of things at school and had got into trouble a few weeks before with a load of dodgy mobile phones. Dean's brother Gussie always had things that he gave us to sell, mostly games and stuff. Not that I was complaining. I needed the money.

'Cool – you got loads?' I asked Dean.

'Nuff . . .' he told me.

'Come on – let's go find Robert and Wesley, I've got some games that they like.'

Robert Sargeant and Wesley Magoogan were in our year and they were into fantasy novels and skater music and stuff. The school nerds. But they always bought games and the selection Dean had with him was exactly the sort they liked.

'Cool,' I said, wondering where Grace and Hannah had gone.

# TWO

Robert and Wesley were talking to some of their friends about the latest fantasy novel that they were reading. It was one of a series of books – *The Dark Lord of Hazelwitch* stories – and they had magicians and goblins and stuff in them. Exactly the sort of book that I hated.

'The ancient Flute of Kings has been taken by Bloodlehart the Great,' Robert was saying as we walked up. I swear he was making it up though. I mean, the names were just stupid and why did all fantasy books have to have magic stones and flutes in them?

'And Princess Wondlebarn is going to have to travel back in time, to before her own birth, to save the people of Hazelwitch . . .' added Wesley as their mates stood and listened.

'But what about Gerafaggan, the Dark Lord?' asked Sailesh Kotecha, one of the nerd posse.

'He's takin' a break, my man,' interrupted Dean. 'He got bored of being evil and that, so he's doing voluntary work with the goblins.'

For a minute I thought that Sailesh had fallen for it, but he hadn't. Instead he tried to diss Dean.

'At least I read,' he said. 'I bet you've never even read a book from start to finish.'

Dean looked at Sailesh like he was shocked and then he looked at me with a grin.

'Read this one book,' he replied, acting serious. ''Bout how this likkle rat-faced bwoi got his head mash up by me.'

Sailesh went red and looked down at his feet.

'You want me to finish *that* book?' asked Dean, only he didn't wait for Sailesh to answer. Instead he smiled at Robert and handed him some games.

'Tek a look at them, my fantasy-reading brother . . . pure warlock business, you get me? An' cheap too . . .'

Robert looked at both of us over his glasses, like we were insects or something, and then he took a look at the games.

'WOW!' he said suddenly, pulling one out and showing it to Wesley.

'EXCELLENT!' agreed Wesley.

I looked at Dean and grinned.

'Spiffing, what?' I said, taking the mickey.

'Four pounds, bro,' said Dean. 'Cheapus Maximus!'

'I'll take it,' said Robert, smiling, and I wondered exactly how many Hazelwitch books there were. In the end I just asked him, as he was getting his dough out.

'Oh, there's seven so far, but that doesn't include the prequels and the two sequels that the author is writing at the same time.'

'You what?' I asked.

'There are going to be two *follow-up* books,' he said slowly.

I looked at him and this red haze started forming in front of my eyes. I thought he was making fun of me and I felt myself getting mad. Then, just as suddenly, I calmed down again. I would have hit him otherwise.

'I know what sequel means,' I replied. 'But how can there be two, *together*?'

Wesley took over. 'The author is writing two alternate sequels and you can choose which one suits your own taste.'

I thought about it for a minute.

'But if there's two sequels, with two different

endings, then the next book ain't gonna make sense . . . the author's gonna have to write another two,' I pointed out.

Wesley grinned like he'd just been snogged by some Hollywood star.

'*Exactly* . . . and then two more and two more and . . .'

'And the whole world is gonna be full up of stupid books about the Dutty Backside of Ganglefart,' said Dean.

Wesley looked at Dean, went bright red, mumbled something about being late for lessons, and walked off. Robert looked at me and then followed his friend, as the rest of the nerd crew dispersed. I asked Dean what we had next.

'Maths,' said Dean. 'Why?'

'I don't think I'm gonna bother,' I said.

'Forget that, bro . . . you'll just get into trouble. What's up, anyway? Things getting funny at home again?' he asked.

'NO!' I shouted.

'Easy, Jit . . . ain't no need to . . .' he began, only I didn't wait around to listen.

Instead I walked off in the direction of the main

doors and walked out into the rain, my head beginning to hurt. I walked round to the side of the school and into the outdoor toilets, locking myself in a cubicle. It took me a few minutes to stop feeling angry and then I started to feel stupid for shouting at my best mate and walking off. But I wouldn't have done it if he hadn't asked me about what was going on at home. It was stressful enough without having to chat about it. Then I remembered how Dean had let me stay at his the last time, and the way his mum had sorted stuff out. I started to get angry again, this time with myself and with Micky. My head was hurting even more and I kicked at the door a few times . . .

Later on I felt all right and I found Dean and Grace in the dinner hall. They were eating and talking about Suky and Imtiaz. When I walked up, Dean just nodded at me and then told me to sit down.

'Easy, bro,' he said, raising his eyebrows.

'Easy,' I replied.

Grace looked at us and then began to ask a question, but I jumped in.

'So what's new with the Suky an' Imi show?' I asked.

'*Well* . . .' began Grace, forgetting what she had

been about to say. 'They're still being really secretive about it all. Everyone knows that they're together but they aren't telling us anything.'

'I can understand that,' said Dean.

'So can I,' I added, although me and Dean had different reasons.

I thought it was to do with Suky being Sikh and Imi being Muslim, but Dean told Grace that the only reason they weren't saying anything was because Grace and Hannah had big gobs.

'That's not true, smelly bum,' replied Grace.

'Yeah it is,' continued Dean. 'You two are like the *Scum* and the *Mirror* combined, only you gossip more than even them papers!'

Grace looked at me and pouted.

'Will you back me up, Jit?' she asked. 'You don't think I'm a gossip, do you?'

I looked at Dean and I wanted to agree with him but I didn't want Grace to get upset, so I just shrugged and said nothing. Which upset her anyway.

'Fat arse,' she said, getting up and walking off with her tray.

'Grace!' I shouted after her but she just turned and stuck her tongue out at me.

'Let her go, bro,' Dean told me, then he grinned.
'One of these days you an' me is gonna go over the
rules when it comes to the ladies.'

'What?' I asked.

'You're actin' like she's really upset but she's just
playin' yer, you get me?'

'No she ain't,' I told him.

Dean shrugged.

'I dunno why you and her don't just get together,
bruv. It's obvious that you like her.'

I looked over at Grace, who was standing chatting
to Hannah. Then I turned back to Dean.

'No I don't,' I told him, which was a lie. I did like
her but I wasn't sure that she liked me, and I didn't
want to mess up by asking her. Besides, she wouldn't
want me anyway.

'What*ever*,' replied Dean, in a high-pitched voice,
pretending to be a girl. 'Don't be coming cryin' to me
when it all hits the fan, girlfriend.'

I looked around us, embarrassed, but no one was
listening. 'You're a weirdo, bro,' I told him.

Dean grinned. 'Look who's talking,' he said.

After school, I had to go home. I asked Grace what she

was doing but she had a birthday party to go to. I thought about going round to Dean's or calling for Hannah but they were both busy too. I walked into the living room, which was still a complete mess, and realized that my mum was out. I sat down on the sofa and turned on the TV, hoping that she'd gone for the night. But I couldn't relax. Everywhere I looked there were empty beer cans and ashtrays and stuff. And the place stank. I got up and went into the kitchen, shaking my head at the pile of dishes in and around the sink, grabbed a bin bag and went back into the living room. It took me nearly two hours to clear up everything, including the dishes, and when I was done I was so tired that I fell asleep on the sofa.

It was gone ten when I woke up. My stomach was rumbling and my head hurt. I looked around and saw that my mum hadn't come home. There was no food in either so I decided to go down to the chippie for the third time that week. I had homework to do for the next day but I decided that it could wait. I was hungry.

# THREE

The next morning I got up early and had a shower. Then I looked around for some clean clothes but my mum hadn't done any washing. I knocked on her bedroom door, waiting to hear her mumble like normal, but this time the door opened and Micky was standing there, his hair all over the place and sleep in his eyes.

'What do yer want?' he hissed.

'Nothing from you . . .' I told him, turning and heading back to my room, where I put on the same clothes that I'd been wearing for the last few days. At least it was Friday. I would be able to wash my uniform over the weekend.

I walked downstairs and made myself some coffee, stepping over the mess that my mum and Micky had left when they'd come in the previous night. So much for tidying up, I thought to myself. As I looked around I saw Micky's jacket. I picked up a can of lager, shook

it to make sure there was something in it, and poured
it over the jacket. Then I sat and watched morning
telly and wondered how I was going to handle the
weekend. I didn't like being at home when Micky was
there and I knew that my mum was off work all weekend, which meant that he would be around all day,
both days. I swore at the thought, took my mug into
the kitchen, washed it, grabbed my bag and left the
house, nearly an hour before I needed to.

I walked to the main road, past the daily traffic jam,
heading to Grace's. I was trying to stop myself from
getting angry about Micky but it wasn't working. I
couldn't believe that my mum had let him back into
the house after everything he had done. I was really
angry with her and if I had known where my dad was,
I would have gone to him. But he didn't want me
either, and I was kind of stuck. So I just got angrier as
I walked, and by the time I reached the row of shops
behind Grace's house, I was so wound up that I had to
sit down on a wall and calm myself. I put my hand in
my pocket and realized that I only had a couple of quid
to my name.

'No!' I said out loud, as a couple of men walked by,
wearing blue overalls.

'Easy, kid,' said one of them, smiling. 'Can't be that bad.'

I shrugged and kicked my feet, wondering how I was going to pay for my bus fare and eat too. I'd just have to pretend to be full at lunch time again, or pick at what Dean ate. It wouldn't be the first time.

I jumped off the wall and went to call for Grace, straightening my hair as much as I could and brushing down my clothes. Her dad answered the door.

'Hello, Jit!' he said with a huge smile.

'Hi, Mr Parkhurst. Is Grace ready to catch the bus yet?'

Grace's dad shook his head.

'No – she's running late so I'm going to give her a lift. Come in – and please, call me Michael.'

'OK,' I replied, following him into their kitchen.

'I'm having a cup of coffee. Would you like one?' he asked me.

I looked over at the gleaming silver coffee machine that he had bought recently and then around the kitchen, which was so clean you could have eaten off the floor. I nodded.

'If there's time,' I said.

Grace's dad grinned again. 'There's always time

where Grace is concerned. I think she's in the shower
. . . come on, let me show you how the machine
works.'

I nodded. Mr Parkhurst had already shown me how
it worked loads of times but he was kind of forgetful
and I liked him so I didn't mention it. Grace appeared
about ten minutes later.

'Hey, Jit! When did you get here?' she asked, looking surprised.

I thought she might think I was mad or something
so I coughed and looked away.

'Got the time wrong,' I told her. 'So I was a bit
early.'

'Never mind!' boomed her dad. 'It meant that we
got to spend some time together, Jit and I.'

Grace grinned. 'So now you're crawling to my dad?'
she asked.

'Er . . .' I began, embarrassed that she thought that.

'*Well?*' she asked.

'No I ain't,' I finished. 'I was just early, that's all.'

She smiled at me and came and sat down.

'It's fine, you silly monkey bum,' she said, touching
my arm.

I felt a shiver run across my chest and I pulled my

arm away. What if she could smell my clothes? I thought. She'd think that I was a tramp. I stood up and tried to change the subject.

'Come on,' I told her, 'we've got to get to school.'

Grace looked at me like I was mad.

'Blimey, *what's up with you*? Are you ill or something?'

'No!' I said quickly.

'I didn't want her to know what was up. I didn't want anyone to know. Dean had found out a bit, a few weeks earlier, but that was a one-off. I could handle my own problems. I didn't want to stress my mates with them too.

'God – I was only *asking* . . .' she said, looking all upset.

'Er . . . I didn't mean . . . I, er . . . come on,' I mumbled, like an idiot.

'OK, people,' said Mr Parkhurst, rescuing me from foot in mouth. 'Time for school.'

I was in a good mood by the time we arrived at school. Mr Parkhurst had invited me over on Saturday night, along with everyone else, because we hadn't been over for dinner for a while. I agreed straight away, jumping at the chance to get away from my mum and

Micky. Grace was happy about it too.

'We can work on the latest issue of the school news-paper,' she said, smiling.

'Is the next one coming up already?' I asked.

The newspaper had started a few months earlier, after our little gang had got into trouble over a scam to do with lunchtime social clubs, all of it caused by Dean. We had to put one together every month and it was OK really.

'*Yeah*,' replied Grace. 'Lots to do, monkey boy.'

I nodded and we got out of her dad's car and walked into school, ten minutes early. I hadn't been on time for ages and as I walked past Mr Singh, my football coach and year head, I was hoping for him to notice. He did, but not in the way that I wanted him to.

'You need to see me straight after registration,' he said to me.

'What?'

'My office, Jit. And if you can't work out why, you've got the next twenty minutes to do just that.'

I shrugged and turned to Grace.

'Dunno what's up with him,' I said.

Grace just shook her head. 'Maybe it's the lesson that you missed yesterday?' she reminded me.

'Er . . . yeah, *maybe*,' I replied.

I didn't say anything else as we walked to our form room. Instead, I was trying to think up a reason for skiving. Something that wouldn't make Mr Singh angry, or lead to a letter for my mum. Not that she'd read it anyway. She'd just get angry and tell me that I was a waste of space. As we walked in, Mrs Dooher was handing out forms for parents to sign, giving permission for us to have our pictures taken. There was a Book Week coming up and we had a couple of authors coming into school. She handed me mine and then told me that I had to see Mr Singh.

'I know, miss,' I told her.

'Are you OK, Jit?' she asked.

I shrugged. 'S'pose,' I said.

She told me to wait until everyone had gone.

'I just want a quick word with you. Nothing heavy.'

'Cool.' I smiled at her, before turning to Dean and the others. 'Easy . . .'

'Yes, bro,' replied Dean.

'You in trouble again?' asked Imi.

'Dunno,' I said.

'You need to stop skiving,' added Hannah. 'We don't want you to get kicked out or nothing.'

I gulped down a load of air. I'd never even thought about that kind of trouble – enough to get excluded. I started to get really worried.

'*Jit's not gonna get thrown out!*' yelled Grace, jumping in.

'OK, OK, Sister Gee!' grinned Dean. 'Ain't no one throwin' yer man out of school!'

I gave Dean a dirty look.

'I *ain't* her man,' I told him.

I heard Hannah mumble something under her breath.

'*You what?*' I asked her.

She grinned at me. 'Oh – nothing,' she replied. 'Just talking to myself.'

'I ain't surprised,' Dean told us. 'No one else talks to her . . . on account of how mad she is.'

'You do talk a lot of nonsense, Han,' Suky told her.

'Least I don't hide under the stairs to kiss my boyfriend,' countered Hannah.

'I *don't*!' replied Suky.

'Yeah, you do,' answered Dean. 'We all seen yer the other day . . . kissin' each other like you was lickin' food off a plate.'

'*URRGH!*' said Grace.

'Get lost!' replied Suky, looking at Imi.

'*Yeah* – get lost,' he said, repeating what Suky had said.

'*Oooh* – check out the *couple*!' laughed Hannah. 'They even say the same things . . . must be love!'

'As long as you don't start wearing her underwear, bro,' Dean said to Imi. 'Them kind of kinkiness can *gwaan*!'

They all burst into laughter, even Imi and Suky. I didn't. I just sat there and watched them, still worried about what Mr Singh was going to say.

# FOUR

First I had to get past Mrs Dooher. I waited around until everyone had left and then I got up and walked over to her desk.

'What did you want to see me about, miss?' I asked her.

'Go and close the door first,' she told me.

When I returned to the table she looked up at me and tried to smile but her face looked disappointed instead. I started to feel angry with myself.

'You know what I'm going to say, don't you?' she asked.

I shrugged.

'You can't just skip lessons whenever you like, Jit. It's not going to be tolerated.'

'Yeah, I know and I'm sorry but I wasn't feeling well and . . .' I started.

Mrs Dooher just shook her head slowly.

'There's always *something*, Jit. There's always an

excuse. But now the other teachers are beginning to realize and, regardless of what you might think, we *do* talk to each other. Maths yesterday was the fourth lesson you've skipped in three weeks, only to turn up later in the day as though we wouldn't notice.'

I didn't know what to say so I nodded.

'Mr Singh isn't angry with you, he's worried. And so am I. We need to find out why you do it.'

'It's nothing really . . . I was just . . . I won't do it again,' I told her.

'That's just it, Jit. We spoke to your primary school and you were doing the same thing there too . . . what is it that makes you skip school?'

I looked away and I could smell my uniform, which made me even more determined not to say anything.

'What's up, Jit?'

'Nuttin',' I replied.

'Come on,' she said in her soft Liverpool accent. 'I wasn't born yesterday . . . I'm here to talk to.'

'But . . .'

It went on like that for another few minutes and then I went off to see Mr Singh, who repeated what Mrs Dooher had said for about half an hour.

Then he looked out of the window of his office.

'I'm going to have to take action,' he said, not looking at me.

'But I said I wouldn't do it again . . .' I protested.

'That's not enough, son. It can't be one rule for you . . . There are procedures we have to take as a school.'

'What – so you're just gonna hang me out to dry like everyone else?' I spat out, instantly wishing that I hadn't said anything.

'Who's hung you out to dry?' he asked, looking at me this time.

'No one . . .' I mumbled.

'Jit?'

'No one, man. Just leave it . . . Ain't like you people care anyways. It's just summat you have to do – that's what you just said, weren't it?'

'No, that's not what I said at all. Why do you think I'm sitting here talking to you?'

I looked at him, shrugged and turned away. 'I dunno . . . maybe 'cos you have to.'

Mr Singh shook his head. 'I'm here because I care about you. I've seen the way you walk from one bit of trouble to another . . . I know that something's wrong. All I'm trying to do is help you.'

'So, what you gonna do?' I asked him.

'Well that depends on you, Jit. I have to write a letter to your mum to tell her what's been going on.'

I wanted to groan but I didn't. My mum never read any letters from school.

'And then maybe we'll get her in and have a chat about things.'

'You can't do that! I blurted. 'I don't want her to come here . . . she's too busy anyways, always at work and that.'

'We can work around that, Jit,' he told me.

He took an envelope that was on his desk and gave it to me.

'That's for your mum. She needs to read it and get in touch with the school. She can call me any time she likes. I do need to talk to her before next Friday however . . . or I'll have to get her to come in.'

I didn't listen to anything else he said. My mum wouldn't call the school, and even if she did, I didn't want to give her the letter anyway. She'd just get angry, and so would Micky, and then he'd make my life even worse and my mum would end up drinking more. I didn't want that. I had to find a way to blag it, only I couldn't work out what that would be.

'Are you listening to me, son?' I heard Singh say.

'Huh?'

He shook his head. 'I was saying that you need to attend your lessons from now on. This is your first real warning, Jit, and you won't get too many more.'

'Yessir,' I replied.

'Right, now sit here until break and then go and join your friends.'

'Thank you, sir,' I said.

'Oh and one more thing, Jit,' he said as he stood up and grabbed his mug of coffee, 'if you *are* excluded you won't be eligible for the football team.'

I looked at him in shock. Football was one of the few reasons that I liked school at all. I couldn't get kicked out of the team. I nodded and told him that I understood.

The rest of the day went by in a haze. I tried to get into what my friends were doing but all I could think about was Singh's warning. It felt like I had the flu – you know, when you can't think clearly and your head feels like it's weighed down with something. It was even worse in our last lesson because I was so hungry. I felt weak and couldn't wait for the day to finish. When it did, I told Grace and Dean that I'd see them the next day and I went home on my own, praying that Micky would be out. But as I opened the front door, I could smell cigarettes and I knew that my prayers hadn't been answered. I walked through to the living room and saw him lying on the sofa, watching some talk show. There were cans of cider on the floor beside the sofa and an overflowing ashtray. The curtains were drawn too and the room was all gloomy.

Not wanting to talk to him, I decided to go straight up to my room but it didn't work.

'You got any money?' he asked me.

'What?'

'Money . . . you deaf or summat?'

I turned to walk up the stairs.

'I'm talkin' to yer, you likkle dick!'

'Get lost!' I told him.

He jumped up and stood over me, trying to look threatening. I looked into his face. I wanted to puke at the smell of his breath. He hadn't shaved and his hair was all lank and greasy.

'You tellin' me to get lost?' he sneered.

'So?' I asked, not wanting him to think I was scared of him.

'You little—'

'You touch me and I'll stab you in the head,' I told him calmly.

'Just give me yer money or I'll throw you out again!' he threatened.

I backed down a bit and looked past him, wishing that my mum had been in to see the way he spoke to me. 'I ain't got no money,' I said. 'And even if I did . . . I wouldn't give you none.'

He sneered for a few seconds and then his eyes went dead and he grabbed the front of my jacket, swearing his head off. He dragged me to the door before I could do anything, opened it and threw me out into the street, slamming it shut behind me. I stood and looked at the door as tears started welling. I tried really hard not to cry but I couldn't help it. I got angry with myself for being so weak and I started kicking the door, over and over again, until I'd hurt my foot. But he didn't open it, and when I tried my key, which I still had, it wouldn't work because he had double locked the door from the inside.

I stood for a while longer and then remembered that my mum was working until ten o'clock. I put my hand in my pocket and found fifty-four pence. Enough to get a packet of crisps. I kicked the door once more and swore at the top of my voice, so loud that my next-door neighbours looked out of their front window. Not that I cared. I did up my jacket, turned towards the main road and set off, not knowing where I was going to go, or what I was going to do until my mum got back.

# FIVE

I walked down the main road towards the shops, watching all the people walking about and the traffic. There were loads of Muslim people around because it was Friday, their main prayer day, and as I walked past the mosque I watched the people standing around chatting, whilst the kids messed about in the car park, running around and stuff. I turned left and headed down a side street, just because I didn't have anything to do. The street was narrow, with cars parked both sides, and ahead of me two Punjabi men were arguing over a parking space outside a greengrocer's. They were swearing at each other and some of the stuff they were saying was well nasty. As I went by they stopped for a few seconds, before one of them, who was wearing a turban, said something about the other one's mum. I left them to it.

Further on I bumped into a couple of lads from school, Dilip and Paresh. They were kicking a ball across the road at each other, in between parked cars.

'Easy, Jit!' Dilip said as I walked up.

'Easy,' I replied. 'What a gwaan?'

'Jus' chillin',' he told me. 'Too wet to go up to the park and that so we's just kickin' about out here.'

'You better make sure you don't hit no car,' I said, with a grin. 'I seen the flat-foot way you kick the ball!'

Dilip grinned back. 'Kiss my ass, man,' he replied, as Paresh crossed the road to join us.

'What you doin' walking the streets anyhow?' asked Dilip.

I shrugged and told about half of the truth. 'Locked out – got time to kill . . . me mum ain't home until half-ten.'

Paresh shook his head. 'That's wack . . . so what you gonna do?'

I shrugged again. 'Whatever, you get me . . . Might go check on my boy Dean.'

'What . . . MC Rhymes Too Lame?' laughed Dilip.

'The self-same bwoi,' I told them.

Dilip looked at his watch and then told me he had to go in. I nodded and walked on, wondering if Dean or Hannah were around.

By the time I walked past the church down on St

Philips Road for the fourth time, it was nine-thirty and I had been walking around in circles for hours. I turned back on myself and headed up the road, back towards my area. I walked by two fried chicken shops, a burger place, three pizza and kebab shops and a Caribbean takeaway, getting hungrier each time. My head was light and it felt like there was nothing in my legs at all. And then I saw my mum heading out of an off-licence. She was in her uniform, wearing a coat over the top of it, and in her hand she had a bag full of booze.

'MUM!' I shouted.

She turned round, saw me and smiled.

'Hey, baby!' she said, embarrassingly.

I walked up to her and she gave me a big hug.

'My baby,' she said about ten times.

I looked at her, realized that she was already drunk, and then hugged her some more.

'Micky didn't let me in,' I told her.

'Huh,' she asked, not really listening.

'Well I let myself in but he was mean to me and then he threw me . . .' I began, only to realize that my mum just wasn't paying any attention at all.

I sighed and let it go. 'You eaten yet, Mum?' I asked.

She shook her head.

'And how come you finished work early?' I asked.

'Dunno . . . who cares anyhow?' she said, smiling. 'You want chips, baby?'

I sighed again and nodded. Four times this week, I thought to myself. Not that I was bothered. I would have eaten a barbecued rat. We walked down the road, towards another fried chicken shop and got some food before heading home. I wondered what Micky would say when he saw me with Mum but I knew that it wouldn't be a problem. There was no way he was going to bully me with Mum around. He was stupid but not *that* stupid. In the end he was sly about it.

'I must have fallen asleep,' he told my mum, as he opened the door. 'I think I double locked it by mistake.'

He gave me a look that told me to keep quiet.

'I'm ever so *sorry*, Jit.'

My mum wasn't listening though. She had opened a bottle of wine and was in the kitchen getting plates for our food. I looked at Micky and smiled. '*Not a word*,' he warned.

'You know – one of these days I'm gonna *get* you,'

I warned back. 'You'll be out cold or have your back turned and I'm gonna do yer.'

'*You effing likkle—*' he began, just as my mum walked in from the kitchen.

'You what?' she asked him, and for a second I hoped that she'd heard him. But she hadn't.

Micky turned on the cheese.

'I was just saying how much I *enjoy* being here with Jit . . . it's like we're *best* mates. Ain't that right, Jit?'

I looked at my mum, back at Micky and pretended to agree.

'Yeah . . . that's right, Mum.'

She smiled, as I sat down to eat my chicken and chips. 'That's so lovely,' she replied. 'No, *really . . .*'

It was midnight when I got my dirty clothes together and put them in the washing machine. My mum and Micky had gone to sleep, leaving the living room a stinking mess. I turned on the machine and tidied up the house, as I waited for the cycle to finish, so that I could put the clothes straight into the dryer. As I waited, I watched late-night telly, getting bored really quickly until I saw a programme about the latest computer games. I sat and watched that for a bit and then some lame film in German, before sorting out my clothes and heading for my bedroom.

As I walked past my mum's room, the door opened and Micky walked out. He smiled at me, grabbed me by the neck and held me against the wall.

'You think you're clever?' he whispered.

I didn't reply. Instead I stared at him, not letting him see that I was in pain. But my eyes were watering again.

'Next time you try and take me for a fool, I'll get really angry . . . and you ain't seen nothing like that, son. I promise.'

He let me go and went to the bathroom. I rubbed my neck, went into my bedroom and locked the door. I was tired but too angry to sleep. I sat up for a few hours and tried to think of a way to get rid of Micky once and for all. It took me ages but in the end I had a brainwave. I actually fell asleep with a smile on my face . . .

I didn't wake up until eleven and when I went downstairs all of my clean clothes had been folded neatly. There was also an envelope on the table with my name on it, written in Mum's handwriting. I opened it.

Inside was a twenty-pound note, and a letter. Mum and Micky had gone away, it told me, and wouldn't be back until the following day. The money was for food and there was a big kiss at the foot of the letter. I sat down, relieved that I wouldn't have to deal with Micky, and thought about how much I didn't want him to be in Mum's life. She was different around him, always smoking and drinking, and I was worried that it was going to make her ill. As I sat and thought about it, I became even more determined to get rid of Micky. My plan was going to take a bit of work, maybe even a bit of help from my mates. Even if I had to let them know how bad things really were, I didn't care. The shame would be worth it if I could get rid of Micky.

# SIX

I was the first one to get to Grace's house, followed five minutes later by Hannah and Dean. I was in her cellar, setting up a game of pool, when they walked in. Dean gave me a funny look.

'We just called for you and you is already here,' he said.

'Yeah – we knocked for ages and no one answered,' said Hannah.

I shrugged. 'You didn't tell me that you were gonna call for me,' I replied.

'Yeah, but we never do,' said Hannah. 'Your mum out or something?'

I nodded. 'Yeah – she's gone away with—'

'She got a new man?' asked Hannah.

I was about to tell her the truth but something in my head stopped me and I told her a lie instead.

'Nah . . . she's with an aunt.'

'Oh, right . . .'

Dean took the cue from my hands and broke off a new game. 'Enough chit-chat – time to get beat at pool by the Number One,' he announced.

Grace looked at Hannah and smirked. 'More like a Number Two,' she said, giggling.

Dean shook his head. 'See how you go on, Sister Gee? And I'm so nice to you too.'

Grace grinned.

'I'm soooo sorry, Deany-Beany-Boy. I didn't mean to upset you,' she teased.

'Yeah – don't have a tantrum,' said Hannah.

'Just watch the master at work,' Dean replied.

Hannah looked at Grace. 'He used to throw tantrums at junior school. Like if he was tryin' to talk to you and you didn't listen – he used to cry like a baby.'

'No! I don't believe you,' replied Grace. 'Not big bad Dean.'

'You two are bad,' I told them.

'Don't bother me, bro,' said Dean. 'Least I grew up. Hannah still goes on like a baby and as for Grace . . .'

'Grace ain't a baby,' I told him.

'You tell him, Jit!' said Grace, smiling at me.

Dean handed me the cue and shook his head slowly.

'You're supposed to back me up,' he told me. 'You'll be wearing skirts next, bro.'

'Oh shut up, you moron,' said Hannah. 'Don't listen to him, Jit – he's just stupid.'

'Least I ain't got a fat ass,' said Dean, winking at me.

Hannah grabbed the cue out of my hands and pointed it at Dean.

'I'm gonna shove this cue right up *your* fat ass!'

'I do wish you'd get over this fixation with Dean's bottom,' said Mr Parkhurst, appearing at the foot of the stairs.

Everyone laughed except Hannah, who went bright red. Grace's dad was always catching her out just as she was threatening Dean. It happened so often that it was getting silly.

'I'm sure that there are therapists who can help,' continued Mr Parkhurst.

'I was only—' began Hannah, going red again.

'Oh, Dad – stop teasing her,' Grace told him.

Mr Parkhurst looked at me and Dean and winked.

'Looks like I've been told,' he said. 'Now who wants to help me sort out dinner?'

I shrugged and looked at Dean, who shook his head.

'I got this disease, Mr Parkhurst,' he replied. 'Summat 'bout how I can't do no housework 'cos it might kill me . . . *Nohelpyitis* or something.'

Grace's dad laughed.

'Sounds nasty,' he said. 'Is it contagious . . . like those spots you seem to get regularly?'

'NAH!!!!!!!!!!!!!!!' I shouted. 'Dissed by the old man!'

'DAD!' shouted Grace, trying not to laugh too much.

Dean shook his head, picked up another cue and went back to playing pool.

'What are we having for dinner?' asked Hannah.

'Sausage and mash,' beamed Grace's dad. 'Made by my own hand.'

'But Hannah and I are vegetarians,' protested Grace.

'Yes, I know that,' replied her dad. 'That's what the veggie sausages are for.'

'Oh, right,' said Grace. 'I like those.'

Hannah looked at Grace. 'Are they nice?' she asked.

'Mmmm!' Grace replied like a little girl.

Dean snorted. 'Surely you shouldn't eat sausages if you're vegetarian,' he said.

'But they're made of soya and stuff,' said Grace. 'There's no meat in them, stinky boy.'

'Yeah – I know that,' said Dean. 'But sausages are

**47**

normally meat, right? So if you were a grass eater – why would you want sausages? I mean – you don't get vegetarian steak and kidney, do yer?'

Grace looked at him like he was mad. 'But that's what we just said . . . that's why they're vegetarian.'

Dean shook his head. 'I just reckon you're desperate to eat meat, only you'll look silly because you're always goin' on about animals and that.'

'God! Sometimes you're so . . .' began Hannah.

'So, instead you eat vegetarian sausages and pretend that they're really made of pork or beef or . . .'

'OK! shouted Grace's dad, grinning even wider. 'Let's just get them cooked, shall we? You can have a debate about them afterwards.'

I looked at Mr Parkhurst and smiled. 'Would you like me to help you?' I asked.

'*Would you like me to help you?*' mimicked Hannah.

'Yeah – can I be *captain licky bum*, sir?' added Grace.

Dean shook his head again and looked at me.

'Witches,' he said. 'You get me?'

By the time Imtiaz and Suky turned up, together, the food was ready. Mr Parkhurst had piled a load of sausages onto two separate plates, one for meat and the other for non-meat. I helped him take everything through to their dining room, which was almost the same size as the whole ground floor of my mum's house. The gang were sitting round the table, waiting, and Dean was teasing Suky. Grace's dad asked him why.

'They're bumping uglies,' Dean told him.

'I'm sorry?' asked Mr Parkhurst, looking confused.

'Dean means that Imi and Suky are going out with each other,' explained Hannah.

Mr Parkhurst smiled. 'Excellent!' he said. 'I always knew there'd be a couple amongst you . . . too much bickering for there not to be,' he said.

I didn't have a clue what he meant but I nodded anyway and smiled. Imi tried to change the subject.

'Where's your mum, Grace?'

'She's away for the weekend with work,' replied Grace.

'Don't change the subject, Lover Bwoi!' shouted Dean.

'Oh shut up!' Suky told him. 'You're such a little boy sometimes.'

'Man,' corrected Dean. 'Ain't no boy sitting here.'

'You looked in the mirror lately?' replied Suky.

'Yeah – unlike you . . . did you even brush your

hair this morning?' countered Dean.

Suky gave him a death stare.

'Enough . . .' said Grace's dad. 'Let's eat before my mountain of mashed potato goes cold.'

He told everyone to help themselves and went to get some gravy.

'Fool!' whispered Suky to Dean.

'Tramp . . .' replied Dean.

'Just eat your food, will you,' Grace told them. 'You can have a fight afterwards.'

Dean shrugged.

'We need to talk to you all later anyway,' said Imi, looking at Suky.

''Bout what?' mumbled Dean, spitting food everywhere.

'URGH!! Dean!' shouted Suky.

'Sorry,' he said, after he'd swallowed what was left.

'Dutty, nasty little bwoi,' said Hannah.

Dean shoved half a sausage into his mouth and chewed it really fast.

'So, what you need?' I asked.

'Just . . . well . . .'

'Lessons in lurrve?' asked Dean, spitting more food out.

'DEAN!' shouted Grace.

'Sorry, Sister Gee,' he said, not meaning it.

'We'll tell you in a bit,' said Suky, looking at me.

I expected her to look away but she didn't. Instead she kept her eyes on mine for another few moments and in the end it was me who looked away.

'This food's great, Mr Parkhurst,' said Hannah, as he returned from the kitchen.

He sat down and piled a load onto his plate. 'Call me Michael, please,' he said.

I saw Dean grin and knew exactly what was coming. 'How ya' doin', Michael Please?'

Grace's dad looked at me, picked up a vegetarian sausage and threw it at Dean, who ducked. The sausage flew past his head and landed on a side table, next to a pair of glasses and a lamp. We all looked at each other in shock and then started laughing.

# SEVEN

Later on, while Hannah and Dean argued over another game of pool, Suky and Imtiaz told me what they wanted. Grace was sitting right next to me and I could feel her thigh against mine. I could even smell the shampoo she had used on her hair. It felt kind of nice to be so close to her but then I began to wonder if my clothes smelled and I got all embarrassed and moved my leg.

'You OK?' asked Grace, looking worried.

'Er . . . yeah – course I am. Why wouldn't I be?'

'Just wondered,' she told me, as Suky sat down.

'Wondered what?' she asked.

'I was wondering what's up with Jit,' Grace told her. 'He keeps trying to get away from me – I'm beginning to think that I smell . . .'

Not wanting her to think that, I told her that she smelled nice.

'*AHH!*' Suky said.

'So what did you want?' I asked her, changing the subject.

'Oh right . . . *that*,' she replied.

Imi came and sat down opposite us, as behind him, Hannah called Dean a rat. Suky looked at Imi and then back at me.

'My mum and dad want to meet Imi,' she said.

'That's lovely!' answered Grace, looking really excited.

'Not exactly,' Imi told us.

I looked at him and knew what was up straight away.

'It's that Sikh–Muslim thing, innit?' I said to him.

He nodded.

'But what's that got to do with the price of boiled tuna?' asked Grace.

'You what?' replied Suky, looking confused.

'Boiled tuna,' repeated Grace. 'Price of . . .'

Suky looked at her like she was mad. 'Yeah . . . right . . . er . . . *anyway* . . .' she began.

'Suky ain't told her parents that I'm Muslim,' Imi admitted.

I shook my head.

'Yeah, but how many Sikh lads are called Imtiaz?'

I asked. 'They prob'ly worked it out from yer name, bro.'

Imi looked straight at Suky instead of answering. She started to go red.

'I . . . er . . . well, I haven't told them Imi's name,' she admitted.

Grace screwed up her nose. 'So what do they think he's called?' she asked. 'Do you just call him the boy-friend?'

'Er . . .' began Suky, only for Imi to take over.

'That's why we need *you* to do us a favour,' he said to me.

'Yeah, and what's that exactly?' I asked, getting sus-picious.

Suky jumped in. 'OK – we may as well tell you. I'm worried that my dad won't like me going out with a Muslim boy so I told them that I was seeing a Sikh lad . . .'

'Called Imtiaz?' asked Grace.

Suky shook her head. 'No – a boy, called Jit . . .'

For a split second what she said didn't kick in but then it hit me.

'YOU WHAT?' I half shouted.

'Er . . . sorry,' replied Suky, looking embarrassed.

'Yeah . . . sorry, bro,' added Imtiaz.

I looked at Grace, who started to grin.

'You told your dad that you were going out with Jit?' she asked.

'Er . . . yeah, I suppose I did,' replied Suky.

'*JIT?*' repeated Grace.

'Yeah – what's the big deal?' Suky asked, playing it cool.

'The thing is . . . Suky's parents are kind of chilled out about her havin' a boyfriend,' Imi told us.

'They think it's cute,' said Suky, looking shamed.

'So, anyway, they're having a get-together next weekend and I'm . . . I mean you're . . .'

I nearly dropped the glass of juice I was holding.

'NAH . . . *no way*! I ain't . . .' I began, only Grace's laughter stopped me.

'It ain't funny, Grace,' I told her.

'WHAT AIN'T?' shouted Dean from behind us.

'Jit . . . goin' out with Suky,' Grace managed to get out.

'EH?' replied Hannah, looking confused. 'But I thought that Imi was going out with . . .'

Dean grinned at me. 'Yes, bro! You is one dark horse!'

'But I ain't goin' out with her,' I protested. Well, I wasn't. And I wouldn't either.

'It's just one evening, Jit,' said Suky. 'Please . . . ?'

I stood up and walked over to the pool table, leaning against it. They were all mad. All of them.

'What happens if they invite me over again?'

'We can cross that bridge when we get to it,' argued Imi.

I shook my head. 'I ain't crossing no bridges, ain't jumping off no cliffs and I ain't pretendin' to be you for Suky's dad.'

'And the rest of her family,' said Imi. 'There's a load of aunts and uncles coming.'

'Yeah, it's my brother's birthday party,' Suky added.

'It still ain't happening,' I told them.

Everyone was quiet by that point and they were all sitting down except for me. I waited for someone else to speak.

'Well I don't see what all the fuss is,' said Hannah. 'I mean – do you *know* that your dad won't like Imtiaz, Suky?'

Suky didn't say anything.

'*Well . . . ?*' I added.

'I just *know*, all right. It's that whole religion thing.

**56**

I mean, even if my dad was chilled about it, and he's pretty cool – the rest of my family wouldn't be happy.'

Grace put her hand up like she was at school and Dean saw her.

'Yes, Miss Parkhurst – anything you'd like to say?' he asked, in a deep voice.

'Yes, sir . . . I was wondering why it was anyone else's business,' said Grace.

Suky sighed.

'Look, it's not the same for you,' she told Grace. 'This is one of those Asian tradition things . . . I don't mean to be rude, Grace, but you just wouldn't understand, OK?'

'You're not being rude,' Grace told her. 'You're just assuming that your dad won't like Imi because he's Muslim – but what if you're *wrong*?'

Suky shook her head. 'I'm not,' she said.

I looked at Dean, who shrugged. Something didn't make sense to me and I said so.

'Why don't you just say that your boyfriend is away with his family?' I asked.

'Yeah – tell them *Jit* is in Birmingham or somewhere,' said Dean.

Imi shook his head this time.

'Used that one already,' he said.

'Yeah, about six times,' added Suky. 'My dad thinks that I've made him up.'

'But you have,' said Dean. 'You *have* made him up, Suky.'

'Well,' said Grace, grinning, 'I think that Jit *should* do it – it'll be *funny*!'

'For you lot maybe,' I said. 'I still ain't doin' it.'

'*Please* . . .' begged Suky. 'It'll be OK . . . honest. It's just one evening!'

'Why should I?' I asked them.

'As a favour to your friends?' suggested Hannah.

I glared at her. '*What* – you in on this too?'

Hannah shrugged. 'I don't see how one evening is gonna make a difference.'

I sighed. 'What happens when they wanna see her boyfriend again?'

'Oh *yeah* . . .' agreed Dean.

'*See*? Finally one of you is getting me.'

'Or *Imi* could go as Jit?' suggested Grace. 'How are your family gonna know he isn't *called* Jit?'

Suky shook her head.

'They know him from school events,' she told us.

'They've met him loads of times.'

'We've been through every option,' said Imi, 'and this is the *only* one.'

I stood where I was and shook my head over and over again.

'I ain't doing it,' I told them.

# EIGHT

The next day I woke up early and decided to make the most of having the house to myself. I went round and tidied up really quickly, had a shower and found some clean clothes. Then I went into the kitchen to see if there was anything to eat. I found a few eggs, some bread and a bit of bacon, so I cooked those and had them with some tea. It was really good not to have Mum and Micky around, complaining about hangovers or telling me to shut up all the time.

Then I went for a walk and bought a newspaper. I'd found some money whilst tidying up. It had been stuck down the back of the sofa and probably belonged to Micky, which made spending it seem even more fun. I walked home and read the sports section, wondering when my stupid footie team would get better. I had the TV on nice and loud, and just for the hell of it, I put Mum's little stereo on too, although her taste in music is lame. It was all to show that I was the boss, although there wasn't anyone around to see it.

But I didn't care. Just being relaxed was enough for me, not wondering all the time about what kind of mood Micky was in. Or worrying about how drunk my mum was. Almost like normal.

I still got bored though, and in the afternoon I decided to call Grace. I picked up the phone, only to find that the line was dead. It wasn't the first time. Micky had probably spent the money on booze or some greyhound at the bookies. My mum was always having to pay for the line to be reconnected. Instead I decided to go round to Hannah's first and try and call Grace from there.

Hannah was half asleep when she answered the door and gave me a funny look when I asked if I could use the phone. Her robe was falling open and I could see her bra, which was pink. I looked away, then back again, and then away once more.

'What's up with yours?' she yawned at me.

'Knackered . . . go on – it's only to call Grace,' I said.

Hannah nodded and led me into the house. There was just one room that led through to the kitchen, just like my mum's, only Hannah's was clean and smelled of flowers, not fag smoke and spilled booze. She pointed at the phone before she spoke.

'OK, but be quiet – Mum's asleep.'

'She been on nights?' I asked, wondering if I should tell Hannah that she was flashing me. But I didn't.

'Yeah . . . your mum too?'

I shook my head. 'Nah she's gone away for the weekend . . . see her brother,' I told her.

Hannah raised an eyebrow.

'You said her sister yesterday,' she replied.

'What?'

'Her sister . . . you said it was her sister.'

I looked away.

'Whatever . . . can I use the phone or not?' I snapped, regretting it straight away.

Hannah was my oldest friend. I'd known her for four days longer than I'd known Dean, and she was used to me being an idiot, I reckon. She didn't get upset, just smiled and told me I was a freak.

'I might come with you,' she yawned.

'Cool . . . but you'd better get dressed . . . yer robe thing is half open,' I told her, trying not to look. Again.

She glanced down, said 'Oops!' and pulled it closed.

'Bet you copped a right eyeful,' she grinned at me.

'Weren't lookin',' I lied.

Hannah pulled a face. 'You're only interested in Grace – is that it?' she said, teasing me.

'*No!*' I said loudly.

'I think my lad doth protest too much,' she said through another yawn.

'You *what*?'

'It's from some play or summat,' she told me.

'Just go get dressed, man, and let me call Grace.'

'Ooh,' replied Hannah, in a French accent. 'Check out Meester Masterful . . . I think I like it, *chéri*.'

We spent the afternoon playing pool and chatting about school, and every ten minutes or so Hannah and Grace asked me why I had been so funny about helping Suky and Imtiaz out. I kept changing the subject, not wanting to go over it again and again, but they didn't let up.

'I just think it's stupid, that's all,' I told them.

'But it'll be a laugh,' Grace told me.

'For *you lot*, maybe . . . What do I know about Suky's dad? What if he don't like me or he finds out the truth?'

Hannah shrugged.

'That's Suky's problem,' she said. 'But you could help her out. We're supposed to be friends, all of us.'

'Yeah, and that's what friends do,' added Grace. 'Help each other.'

'I still ain't doin' it,' I told them.

Grace shook her head. 'What if *you* need help one day?'

'I don't,' I said.

'Yeah, but what if you did?' she repeated, only I wasn't really listening.

Instead I was trying to think of my plan to get rid of Micky, and about how I was an idiot because I probably *would* need my friends to help me. I didn't let on to Hannah and Grace though. I wanted to think about Suky's idea a bit more first. I shrugged.

'OK then – let me think about it,' I told them.

'YEAH!!!' Grace grinned. 'You'll be the nicest, loveliest boy in the whole school if you help them.'

'Yeah – and you'll get so much good karma you'll come back as a very rich man,' added Hannah.

I didn't have a clue what she was on about. 'Eh?'

'Karma . . . good energy. It's from Buddhism,' explained Hannah.

'Yeah – like reincarnation,' agreed Grace. 'If you're nice in this life you'll be reborn into a better one.'

'You know what – there's crackheads round my way that don't talk as much madness as you two,' I replied.

'*Ooh!* Wanna be careful – being mean – that's bad karma,' said Hannah.

'That's at least five thousand points lost,' added Grace. 'You've just dropped from a possible king to a rabbit.'

Hannah grinned. 'Even worse. I reckon you're gonna come back as a politician . . . all cheesy and greasy and lyin' all the time.'

'A fate worse than *death*,' agreed Grace.

'*Much worse*,' added Hannah.

'Like the worst thing that you can think of – times a *billion*,' said Grace.

'*Worse City* . . . the streets where things can't get any . . .' began Hannah.

'*Worse*,' finished Grace.

I just sat where I was and shook my head at them. They were nuts.

Later on, when I got in, I realized that I was going to need all the help I could get. My mum and Micky were back and they were sitting on the sofa waiting for me when I walked in. My mum smiled at me and told me to sit down. Micky shifted along so that I could sit next to him but I stayed where I was.

'What?' I asked, when she told me she had something important to tell me.

'We're going to get married,' she said.

My stomach turned over and I felt sweat breaking on my forehead.

'Well?' she asked.

I nodded because that was all I could manage. My head was spinning. Micky looked at me with his stupid grin and I could see it in his eyes – what was going through his mind. *I've got you now, you little freak. I win . . .*

I felt the urge to throw up and tried to force it back.

'But . . .' I heard myself saying.

'He's going to move back in with us, baby . . . you've been getting on so well together. It'll be like a fresh start. A new family – won't it, Micky?' my mum said.

Micky grinned even wider.

'I told yer mam how we've got an understandin' now, Jit. Ain't that right . . . you an' me – we're like bestest mates, in't we?' he told me.

I couldn't think, couldn't speak. Instead I mumbled that I wasn't feeling well and ran upstairs to my room, my head spinning. He'd done it. Got his way, like the rat that he was, and now I was gonna be stuck with him. Like he was trying to prove it, Micky walked into my room without knocking.

'Get out,' I told him.

'Now, now, son – no need for that. I'm gonna be here all the time and we're gonna have to get on,' he sneered.

I told him to get lost but he walked over to my bed and grabbed me by the throat again. His face was red and his eyes were bloodshot. I could smell his breath too, and if he hadn't been trying to strangle me, I would have thrown up because it smelled so bad.

''Cos if we don't, he spat in a whisper, 'I'm gonna have to teach you a few lessons . . . understand?'

# NINE

'I'll do it,' I told Suky the following Wednesday, as we were sitting watching the rain falling outside during lunch time.

'What?' she asked, looking surprised.

'Your thing – 'bout being yer boyfriend for yer family . . . I'll do it,' I explained.

I thought she would thank me and say that I was a good friend or something, but instead she jumped up and gave me a hug and a kiss, just as Grace came walking up to us.

'You're *sooo* lovely – I *lurvve* you!' she screamed.

I pushed her away and looked at Grace, feeling guilty. Then I started to get mad at myself for feeling that way and I had to count to ten, like Mr Singh had taught me in football, to calm myself down. When I'd finished I turned to Suky.

'There's no need to cover me in spit though, is there?' I said to her, smiling a bit.

'Am I interrupting something?' asked Grace, with a strange look on her face that I couldn't work out.

'No . . . I was just—' I began, only Suky grabbed me again.

'He was just saying how wonderful he is and how much he's gonna help me and Imi out!' she told Grace, before kissing me again.

'Gerroff!' I replied, pushing her away again.

Grace gave me another funny look and then sat down on a radiator. 'Well, that's nice,' she said.

'We'll have to get together before Saturday to go over a few things,' continued Suky.

'Like what?' Grace and me asked at the same time.

'Like *stuff*,' replied Suky, as if that made it clearer.

'What stuff?' I asked again.

'The things that a boyfriend is supposed to know . . . like what size feet I've got and my birthday and things,' she told me.

'But does Imi know what size feet you've got?' I asked her.

'That's not the point,' she replied. 'You've gotta know things about me – just in case my family ask you.'

'But why would they ask me?' I said, confused.

Suky grinned.

'You don't know my family . . . they're like proper secret agents. They'll ask you *loads* of stuff.'

I groaned. It was bad enough having to do it in the first place. I didn't want to have to sit through a test as well. I had school for that.

'And, besides . . .' said Suky, looking a bit shady, 'I've kind of told them what your dad does for a living.'

'But *I* don't know what my dad does,' I reminded her. 'I never see my—'

'So, *anyway*, I told them that he's a businessman – owns a load of shops. They liked that . . .' she butted in.

'That's a bit naughty,' said Grace.

'Naughty? That's just stupid! I don't look like some-one whose dad is rich,' I complained.

'Oh, that don't matter,' said Suky, before realizing what she'd done and going a bit red. 'I'm sorry – I never meant to . . .'

''S OK,' I told her.

'So we can meet up somewhere – after school?'

I looked at Grace, not knowing why, and then back at Suky. I shrugged.

'OK then! We'll meet up after school and go and get a coffee or something.'

'And I can come too!' beamed Grace. 'It'll be fun.'

Suky shook her head. 'Why do you need to be there? Just me and Jit . . . Otherwise we'll end up talking rubbish like we always do when we get together.'

Grace's face fell and she looked at me. I think I was supposed to say that she could come along too, but instead I just shrugged.

'*Fine!*' she said, walking off.

'*Great!*' said Suky.

'What?'

'Well she's all *mardy-bum* now.'

I should have gone after Grace or said something but all I did was shrug. I was wondering when to mention that I needed a favour too. In the end I decided that I would speak to Dean first and see what happened after that. I told Suzy I'd see her after school and went off to find Dean.

I found him talking to Wesley and Robert, trying to sell them a load more stuff. They were giving him the latest news on the Dark Lord.

'. . . We were checking the website just last night,' Robert was saying as I reached them. 'The two sequels are done. The author thinks that they are due to come out in time for Christmas.

'Yes – which means that as well as getting myself *The Beginner's Guide to Hazelwitch* and the board game, I can also get two stories . . .'

'Man, you're gonna have a fantasy-filled Christmas,' laughed Dean, before turning to me. 'Whaddya think,' Jit?'

I nodded. 'Yeah – great . . . not my idea of a fun Christmas though,' I said.

'Yeah, an' wass all dat *Beginner's Guide* stuff, bro?' Dean asked Wesley.

'Oh, that! It's exactly what it says – a guide to the magical world of Hazelwitch and all the characters,' replied Wesley.

'But you two know everything about it already,' I pointed out.

'Yeah – I bet you even know what Princess Wondlebarn's bra size is!' laughed Dean.

Wesley and Robert looked at each other in confusion. 'I'm not sure that it goes into *that* much detail,' said Robert.

'What? You don't get to see the Princess in her underwear . . . that's harsh, you get me?' I said.

'But . . . I'm not sure that I'd want to see—' began Robert.

'Yeah, but didn't you say that she looks like Catwoman?' asked Dean.

'In my head . . . yes,' admitted Robert.

'An' when you're lyin' in yer bed at home, feelin' all teenage and that – you tellin' me you don't picture her in her underwear or even less, bro?'

'Erm . . .'

''Cos dat would make you a liar, Roberto, and if yer lyin', well then yer flyin',' finished Dean.

'I'm not . . . I wouldn't . . .' stammered Robert but I started to feel sorry for him so I told Dean to leave it.

'He's only having a laugh with you,' I told Robert and Wesley.

Wesley nodded. 'We know,' he said. 'But it's a damn sight more interesting locking horns with you two than most of the others.'

I didn't really get him but I nodded anyway – like I did in most of my Maths lessons, when in my head I was like Homer Simpson thinking about doughnuts or something, and not what was on the board.

'Yes . . . most of the other bull . . . I mean boys, just beat us up,' added Robert, looking kind of sad.

'Yes,' agreed Wesley, 'you two are kind compared to them.'

I nodded and told Wesley and Robert that we'd see them later.

'I wanna ask you summat,' I told Dean.

Dean watched Wesley and Robert walk away like he was a crocodile watching his prey.

'But I was about to mek some money!' he protested.

'Later, man. I need your help,' I told him.

That got his attention and he asked what was wrong.

'Some of them older lads bothering you?' he asked me.

I shook my head. The older bullies were the least of my worries. I had one of my own at home and I wanted rid of him. But I didn't know how to start telling Dean. He knew that Micky had played up the first time. Dean's mum had let me stay and talked to my mum, who threw Micky out and promised me that he'd never come back. But somehow, Micky wormed his way back in and now he was ten times worse than before. And I was too embarrassed to tell Dean about it. Only I didn't really have a choice any more and if any of my mates were gonna help me without even blinking, it would be Dean.

'I got a serious problem,' I told him.

His face clouded over and he sat down on the stairs that led up to English.

'What's up?' he asked.

'I need your help to ... I gotta ... I ... Look, I need your help to get rid of my mum's boyfriend ...'

# TEN

I explained what was going on with Micky to Dean and he got really angry. He wanted to talk to his mum again but I told him to forget about it.

'It'll just cause more grief and anyway your mum helped out last time and he still came back,' I told him.

'Yeah, but surely your mum can see what's happening?' he said.

'She doesn't see a thing – that's what makes me so angry. It's like he's playing a game and he's good at it. It's all smiles when Mum's around and then when she's out of the way his real personality comes through.'

'I still can't believe she don't know,' he said, shaking his head.

I wondered whether I should tell him about her drink problem. I didn't want to, but in the end I decided that I had to. It would make her reactions easier to understand.

'Er . . . my mum – she's got a problem,' I said.

'I'll say, bro,' agreed Dean.

'Nah – you don't get it. She's got a drink problem . . . they're always drunk when they're together.'

'Serious?' he asked.

'Yeah . . . I mean she goes to work and that but—' A couple of girls from our class walked by so I lowered my voice. 'But she's definitely got a problem.'

Dean shook his head.

'I'm sorry, bro – I dunno what to say,' he told me.

'Just help me with my plan,' I replied. 'I can handle my mum – it's just Micky I need to get rid of.'

Dean looked puzzled. 'So how we gonna do that – kidnap him?' he asked.

I shook my head.

'Nah – nuttin' like that.'

And then I told him my plan.

Mr Singh caught me later on the same day, between the last two lessons. He asked me if I'd given my mum the letter.

'Er . . . yeah, I have . . . she said she'd call you on Friday.'

I hadn't shown her the letter at all. It was still in my bag but I had to think of an excuse quickly so that Singh wouldn't get angry.

'She can't call until about three-ish – is that OK?' I said.

'Well it's a bit late but . . .' he began.

'She don't finish work until then so . . .'

'Doesn't, Jit. She doesn't finish work.'

I shrugged. 'That's what I said, weren't it?'

Mr Singh sighed and took a swig from the mug of coffee he was carrying.

'Never mind . . . just make sure that she does call and then come and see me before you leave school on Friday – do I make myself clear?' he said.

I nodded. But I didn't have any intention of hanging around on Friday afternoon. By the time he'd realized my mum wasn't going to call, I'd be long gone. That way I could deal with the problem the following Monday – once I'd helped Suky out and got the others to help with my plan too. Mr Singh and his letter could wait.

'Now get to your lesson and don't forget football practice is tomorrow after school,' he said.

'Yessir,' I replied, heading off for English.

When I got to the classroom Grace was waiting for me. We always sat at the same table and she was pretending to read something when I walked over.

'You all right?' I asked.

'Hmm?'

'Are you OK?' I repeated.

She looked up from her book and nodded.

'Why wouldn't I be?' she snapped.

I was going to say something but I didn't want to upset her. I couldn't work out why she was angry either, so I shrugged.

'No reason,' I told her, sitting down.

She turned away from me and carried on reading. There was definitely something up with her. I looked at the book she was reading and laughed.

'It's upside down, Grace,' I told her.

'Isn't!' she said quickly.

'Grace . . .! The book is the wrong way round.'

She turned the book round and smiled.

'I was just practising my upside-down reading,' she told me.

'Yeah – and why's that?' I asked, grinning.

'Why not – I might be trapped in a small, locked room one day, and the only instructions on getting out might be stuck to the ceiling. Only I won't be able to move, as I'm tied up, and I'll have to read it all upside down and—'

'Grace?'

'Hmm?'

'Will you just shut up and tell me what's wrong with you?' I said.

She closed the book and put it down.

'Nothing,' she said.

'Why don't you share your conversation with the rest of the class?' said Mr Herbert.

''Cos it's private, you weirdo,' I said quietly.

'WHAT DID YOU SAY, KOONER?' he shouted, going all red in the face.

'He called you a weirdo, sir,' squealed a lad called David.

I spun round and glared at the grass.

'*Yeah?*' said David.

'I'm gonna *batter* you,' I told him, getting out of my chair.

David sat back, looking all worried. Then he started squealing again.

'*Sir! Sir!*'

Herbert told me to sit down about four times before he came over and stood in front of me.

'This is the last time I'm going to ask you!' he told me.

'*And then what?*' I asked him. 'You gonna use those skinny little arms to make me sit down?'

In my head, Herbert's face changed into Micky's and I wanted to punch it but I stayed where I was.

'*RIGHT!* Get out . . .! Now!' shouted Herbert, his voice getting higher as he shouted.

My mind clicked back into the room and I saw Herbert's red face and the giant boil he had on the end of his nose. I started laughing and walked out of the room. In the corridor, Herbert told me that he wasn't going to tolerate my bad behaviour any more.

'I'm going to report you to Mr Singh,' he said.

'You wanna do that on Friday,' I told him, grinning.

'I'm sorry, young man?'

'Don't be,' I told him, noticing the other kids looking through the glass in the door. 'Ain't your fault you were born ugly.'

I thought about how much trouble I was going to be in and then I told myself it didn't matter, and I walked off towards Mr Singh's office.

I got the usual grief from Mr Singh but then he asked me if everything was OK at home. I started wondering what he knew and how, and then I just clammed up and said nothing. In the end he let me go and said that he was going to have to have a serious chat with my mum on Friday when she rang. By the time I met Suky after school, it was all I could think about, and I didn't really pay her much attention.

'You're not listening,' she said, as we sat in a little café near her house.

'What?'

'*See?* Is something wrong, Jit?' she asked.

I shook my head. 'Nah – just the usual.'

Suky gave me a funny look. 'How come you always get into trouble? I mean you aren't stupid but you always manage to upset the teachers.'

'It's my one skill,' I joked.

'*Jit . . .*'

'It's just Herbert – he's got it in for me,' I said, repeating what I had said to Mr Singh.

'That's rubbish!' she replied.

I looked out of the window.

'Just tell me what I need to know,' I told her.

'Sometimes you can be a right freak,' she said, before smiling.

She told me all about her family and warned me that her dad would ask me loads of questions about mine. The one that Suky had made up for me, that is.

'Oh, and my grandmother is a bit senile,' she told me.

'*Great . . .*'

'And she might ask you loads of really weird stuff.'

'Like what?' I asked.

'Dunno. She just might, so be prepared . . .' Suky replied.

'You want me to wear a *turban* an' all?' I joked. 'Pretend that I'm a good Sikh boy and that?'

She grinned at me.

'Idiot.'

I looked at her and smiled.

'There's summat I need from you too,' I told her.

'*What?*' she asked, raising her eyebrows.

'Just summat. I'll tell you all about it at the weekend.'

'Ooh, mystery boy!' she said, laughing afterwards.

'You'll see,' I told her, looking forward to our little arrangement. The more I thought about it, the more it seemed like it would be a laugh. Just what I needed.

# ELEVEN

The rest of the week went by without anything happening and on the Friday afternoon I got out of school as soon as the final bell went, hoping that Mr Singh wouldn't see me. He didn't because he was too busy chatting up Miss Khan, another of our teachers, and I managed to get on the bus behind his back. All the way home I was worried that he might turn up at the house, asking to see my mum, but he would have had a job. She was working the night shift and when I got in she was just on her way out.

'Ain't you a bit early?' I asked, knowing that her shift didn't start until nine o'clock.

'Just gotta do some stuff, baby,' she replied, smiling.

She looked all tired and drawn and there were lines around her eyes. I wanted to tell her to stay at home, to take the night off. Not because I thought she was ill. I just didn't want to be on my own with Micky.

'I'm going to see a friend and then I'm getting a lift from Sarah,' she added.

'Oh . . .' Sarah was Hannah's mum.

'I've left you some stuff for dinner and Micky's got money if you want to get a kebab or something.'

'Cool,' I replied, realizing that I was going to have to get my own food.

'You been OK?' she asked me, ruffling my hair.

'Mum . . .'

'Everything good at school?'

I shrugged. 'Usual,' I told her.

'OK . . . I'd better go. I'll see you tomorrow, baby.'

She kissed me on the cheek and I could smell the alcohol on her breath. Not much, but enough to know that she'd been drinking.

'Mum?' I began, thinking that I would say something about the booze, only I lost my bottle.

'Yeah?'

I shrugged again. 'Nuttin'. Have a good time at work.'

She grinned at me.

'Yeah, right. I'll sing like the dwarfs in *Snow White* whilst I'm stacking canned carrots. You used to love that film when you were a baby.'

'I've grown up a bit since then,' I told her.

She gave me a hug, told me to be good and walked out of the door. I went into the living room and dumped my bag, before heading for my room. I came down just after six and went into the kitchen, where Micky was on the phone to someone.

'*Yeah . . . she's at work. Come roun' when yer like. Me casa is you casa an' all that,*' I heard him say.

He saw me and winked, putting the phone down.

'Awright?'

'When did the phone get put back on?' I asked him.

'Yesterday,' he replied.

'An' I suppose Mum paid for it – *again?*'

'None of yer business . . . we're getting *married* so we share everythin'. Just happens that she's workin' and I ain't.'

I gave him a dirty look and opened the fridge. He picked up a can of lager and cracked it open.

'I got a few mates comin' over tonight so don't get in me way,' he told me.

'*Can I at least get some food first?*' I snapped.

'Do what yer like but don't be askin' me for no money . . . I'm *skint*,' he said.

'But mum said she gave you some dough,' I told him.

He sneered at me. 'None of yer business that, my son. Now eat yer dinner and get lost before I get angry.'

I was going to say something but decided against it. Instead, I rang Dean and asked him if I could stay over. He said that was cool and told me that he wanted to talk to me anyway. I rang off and made myself some fried eggs on toast, with two slices of old-looking bacon and a potato waffle. I ate in the kitchen too, standing up, and then washed the dishes, most of which weren't mine. Then I went up to my room and changed into my normal clothes. My uniform was dirty again but I didn't have time to wash it. I threw it on the floor and decided that I would sort it out in the morning.

Back downstairs, I pulled up the hood of my top, picked up the bag I'd put my change of clothes and toothbrush in, and told Micky where I was going.

'I don't care if yer goin' to the moon,' he replied, opening another can.

I swore at him under my breath and left the house.

\* \* \*

Dean's family were eating when I got there and I had some food too, even though I'd eaten at home. His mum insisted and then his granddad told me that I was too skinny and needed to eat more.

'Look how yuh trousers hangin' off yuh raas, bwoi . . .' he said.

Later, Dean jumped on his bed and told me to grab a chair. I sat at his desk.

'You wanna play Xbox?' he asked.

I nodded. 'In a bit . . . can I play on that new game you got too?'

Dean grinned.

'*Me casa su casa* . . .' he said.

'Micky said that earlier . . . what's it mean?' I asked.

Dean shrugged.

'Like, my house is your house or my girl is your girl or summat.'

'Ain't gonna be *gal*, is it?' I told him.

'True. I wouldn't share none of my girl wit' no one.'

I grinned. 'You ain't got a girl, you fool.'

Dean jumped off the bed and grabbed his mobile. It was the same as the last one I'd had, only I'd sold mine because I needed the money.

'Is all *you* know, innit. Check out these digits, bwoi.'

I looked at the screen and saw the name Monica, a girl who was in the year above us.

'Don't mean it's her number,' I said, secretly jealous. Monica was fit.

'*Yeah, that's right, Dwight.* Like I'm really gonna just put her name and digits in deh for a blag.'

I looked at his face and saw the grin trying to break through.

'That's *exactly* what you done, innit?' I said, shaking my head. 'You ain't right in the brain, geezer, you get me?'

Dean pushed the dial button, holding his finger to his lips, telling me to keep quiet.

'*Yeah,*' he said, before lowering his voice. '*Er . . . YOW! Dat Monica? . . . Yeah, it's D. Got my likkle innocent mate here don't believe this is your number . . . Yeah, dat skinny raas Asian brother . . .*'

Dean covered the mouthpiece, looked at me and mouthed the word 'shame'.

'What, man – what's she sayin'?' I asked, getting annoyed.

Dean held his fingers to his lips again. '*What . . . ? You wanna speak to him, yeah? You got a girl for him too . . . ? Yeah, I think he'll go for that . . .*'

He held out the phone for me. 'Monica wanna talk to *you*,' he said.

I felt butterflies in my stomach and I tried to think of something to say but I couldn't. Dean grinned and thrust the phone into my hands. I put it to my ear.

'Er . . . hi . . . I mean . . . hello? Hello . . . ?'

Only there was no one on the other end.

'*MOVE WITH DAT!!!*' laughed Dean, falling down on his bed because he was laughing so much.

'You stupid—'

'Yuh get *blagged*, bro. *Big* time . . .' He grinned.

I shook my head but couldn't help smiling. He'd got me with a beauty and I knew it.

'I'm just gonna have to kick yer ass at that new game,' I told him.

'Forget that. You could beat me a *thousand* times but it ain't gonna kill the shame you feelin' . . . Yuh get scammed, blood. Well an' *proper*.'

I looked at his phone, then threw it at his head. He caught it and grinned.

Later on, after I'd given him a kicking on his PlayStation, we sat and chatted about my plan to get rid of Micky. I was determined it would work, but Dean wasn't so sure.

'How you gonna get him to do it?' he asked.

'Easy . . . I'm just gonna wind him up. He gets angry even when I don't. If I have a proper go at him, he'll snap.'

'Yeah, but that's *dangerous*, man. What if he hurts you?' he added.

I shrugged.

'Don't care . . . as long as he falls for it. It's the only way Mum will go for it. She won't believe me no other way,' I told him.

'So why do you need *everyone* involved?'

'*Witnesses*,' I replied. 'The more, the better.'

'I ain't too sure about this,' admitted Dean.

'It'll work . . . I'll make *sure* it does,' I insisted.

He gave me a funny look.

'You know, we could just tell my parents. If you think my mum is tough – wait till you see my *dad* get worked up.'

I thanked him for suggesting it but still said no.

'We're gonna be like the Scooby-Doo gang,' said Dean. 'Unmasking the demon.'

'Exactly,' I told him. 'An' by the time I've done with

him – he ain't gonna be able to blag his way out either . . .'

'Forget that dude who wrote that Hazelwitch book. *We* should write 'em,' replied Dean.

# TWELVE

I got home about half eight in the morning, after telling Dean that I needed to do a load of stuff. His mum made me stay long enough for breakfast and made porridge, bacon, scrambled eggs and toast. By the time I got out of Dean's house, I was stuffed. I walked down to the main road and round the corner to my own street. It was cold and the cars had a layer of frost on them. I shivered as I let myself into the house and the smell of stale booze and cigarettes hit me in the face.

The place was a tip again. In the living room were about twenty empty cans of lager, three ashtrays that were so full that the contents had spilled out onto the floor and a load of silver takeaway trays, some of them still half full of Indian food. I drew open the curtains to let some light in, and despite the cold, opened all the windows. Then I removed a load of empty cans from the sofa and one of the ashtrays, and sat down.

I watched telly for a bit and then got up to see if the kitchen was as bad as the living room. It was worse. There was takeaway stuff everywhere and someone had spilled curry on the worktop, all over the chopping board and down the front of one of the cupboards. There was a strange smell coming from somewhere but I couldn't work out where. It was a bitter smell with an edge of bad eggs. I turned and looked in the sink and nearly threw up. Someone had puked all over the dishes and just left it.

I thought about waking my mum up, to show her what Micky and his mates had done, but I stopped myself. She would be tired and fast asleep anyway. Instead I got out some rubber gloves and started to clear everything up. Again. I ran the tap and tried to let as much of the puke rinse away as I could. It took a while and there were bits of food in it. I nearly added my own vomit to it twice but managed to hold it back. Then I washed off the dishes in the sink, glad to see the last bits of puke disappear down the plughole.

By the time I'd finished tidying up Micky's mess it was nearly eleven, and I realized that I hadn't decided what I was going to wear to Suky's house. I went up to my bedroom and rooted through my clothes, most of which needed to be washed. I grabbed my uniform and two shirts and put them in an old basket that my mum used for laundry – not that she had done any recently. In the bathroom I found a load more stuff, most of it my mum's and Micky's. I sorted through it and separated my mum's stuff, which was mainly under-wear, from Micky's dirty clothes, which I threw back on the floor and stood on. I found a pair of his boxer shorts lying on the floor too and, using the end of the loo brush, I picked them up, opened the bathroom window, and threw them out. They caught on the wind and flew over into the neighbours' garden, land-ing on their dustbin.

Back downstairs, I opened the washing-machine door and shoved the clothes in. But then something caught my eye. I saw a pair of women's knickers that were way too big to be my mum's. From doing the washing all the time, I knew my mum was a size ten. These pants were huge – definitely not my mum's, although I didn't want to check the size of them. And then I found a huge bra too, which was a dirty grey colour, but I think was supposed to be white. I stopped what I was doing and looked at them, wondering who they belonged to.

That was when it hit me. Micky was having an affair. He had to be.

I found a plastic carrier bag and shoved the strange underwear into it, ran upstairs and hid it in my room. Then I went back downstairs, just before Micky walked into the kitchen behind me.

'What you doin', yer freak?' he yawned.

'Clearing up your mess,' I told him.

'Good . . . 'bout time you started earning yer keep,' he said.

'Have a good time with your *mates*?' I asked.

He opened the fridge and pulled out a can of lager, opened it and took a big swig. Then he belched and farted at the same time, the dirty scumbag.

'None of yer business,' he replied.

'Will be soon,' I mumbled.

'You *what*?'

'Nuttin',' I replied quickly.

'Better not be,' he said, heading into the living room.

I put the powder in the washing machine and turned it on. Then I stood and thought about what I had just found. I couldn't believe that Micky had been inviting some other woman round when my mum was at work. I started getting angry at first but then I realized that I didn't have any proof apart from some underwear, and Micky could probably blag his way out of that. He was good at it. I had to find more proof. I stood and though about how I was going to do that for about half an hour, only stopping when Micky walked back into the kitchen.

'You mad or summat?' he asked.

'Huh?'

'I said are you off yer head, son? Standin' around like a statue?'

'Just thinking,' I replied. 'You know, that stuff *you* could do if you *had* a brain?'

For a second I thought that he was going to hit me but he just stood where he was, scowling.

'I ain't got no time for you today . . . just keep out of my way,' he snarled.

'Yeah, whatever . . . just go clean yer teeth, you gum-disease-ridden rat,' I said quietly.

'*WHAT?*'

'Something wrong?' asked my mum from the door.

I looked at Micky and grinned. He glared at me for a second or two longer and then turned to my mum with his stupid grin.

'Oh, no . . . Just a joke Jit was tellin' me. Ain't that *right*, son?'

I shrugged. 'If yer like,' I said, before turning to my mum.

'What time did you finish last night?' I asked her.

'About six this morning,' she said.

'You must be knackered . . . go back to bed.'

She shook her head through a yawn.

'Can't. I'm goin' up town with a friend at two. Got to get a dress for a party,' she told me, looking around the kitchen. 'You cleaned up in here?' she added.

I nodded.

'*Ahhh* – aren't you a good lad . . . you didn't have to. I would have done it later.'

'Nah – it's OK. It was like a pig sty in here,' I said.

'Yeah – sorry 'bout that, son,' said Micky, jumping in quickly. 'That was me mates. I'll give 'em a talking to later.'

'No problem,' my mum told him. 'It was a *party* . . . these things happen.'

I didn't reply. Instead I walked out of the kitchen and went and sat on the sofa, changing the channel from some racing programme to a kid's thing. Micky came in after me.

'I were watchin' that,' he told me, as my mum came and sat down next to me.

'*So?*' I replied. 'Now *I'm* watching *this.*'

'*Jit,*' warned my mum.

'Well – ain't he got a job he can do or summat?' I asked.

'That's not fair,' began my mum, only for Saint Micky to step in.

'It's OK, love . . . He's not harmin' nobody. No problem.'

My mum said something about Micky being really good with me, and that was it. I threw the remote at the TV and stormed off to my room.

I came down again around half past three and Micky was asleep on the sofa, snoring. He'd already had a few cans of lager and passed out in front of the racing on the telly. There was a newspaper open and one of the ashtrays was nearly full again. I overcame the urge to kick him in the head as he lay there, and instead I did what I had planned whilst I'd been in my room. Moving around the room quietly, I looked for his mobile phone, which I found in his jacket pocket along with a tenner. I pocketed the money and took his phone into the kitchen. I opened the back door and went into the yard, wondering if the neighbours had found Micky's boxers yet.

The phone battery was low so I checked it quickly. There were a load of names on there, one or two belonging to women, but I still had no proof. I switched into his text message inbox and scanned that instead. As soon as it opened, I saw her name. Tracey. There were about twenty messages from her, broken up now and again with ones from my mum and a few other people. I read the last message, which had been sent earlier that morning: Thnx 4 lst nite. Shme I had 2 go so erly. xxx

I looked through the living-room window and saw that Micky was still asleep. Next I went into his 'sent messages'. I found a text Micky had sent to Tracey the night before, telling her that the coast was clear. I rechecked his inbox and read some of the others Tracey had sent, realizing that I had been right. As I stood and thought hard about what I'd found out, I had a brain-wave. Back indoors, I grabbed the landline phone and dialled Dean's number. Micky stirred a bit, mumbled to himself and went back to snoring.

'Got yer . . .' I said quietly.

# THIRTEEN

Dean told me to be quiet as I walked into his parents' kitchen.

'Gramps is asleep on the sofa and if you wake him up he's gonna complain all day.'

'OK,' I whispered.

Dean closed the kitchen door behind us and asked me if I wanted a drink.

'You got any juice?' I asked.

'You kidding? I got orange, cranberry, pineapple, orange-and-pineapple, red grapefruit, grape . . .'

'That's a whole heap of juice, bro.'

'It's my dad – he loves his juice – only drinks that and water. And the odd brandy now and then.'

'Er . . . I dunno which one to have.'

Dean grabbed the cranberry and orange cartons and made me a mix of the two.

'Try that, bro. It's rude . . .'

I drank the juice as Dean poured himself some. He

took a swig and then asked if I was *sure* that Micky was having an affair.

'Definitely. I found some underwear that don't belong to my mum,' I said.

Dean screwed up his face.

'You know what? I'm a bit freaked out by the fact that you know what size underwear yer mum wears,' he said.

'If you did any housework, you wouldn't care less,' I replied.

'Yeah, but you gotta admit it's not normal,' he continued.

I shrugged. 'I ain't embarrassed. My mum is always busy so I do the washing. Ain't no big deal.'

Dean looked away.

'I don't mean to take the pi—' he began.

'It's OK,' I told him. 'I don't mind.'

He took another swig of his juice before he spoke.

'So, you found some underwear and a load of texts?'

'Yeah . . . some of them are really nasty too . . . you know, explicit and that?' I told him.

He nodded.

'So, did you bring the sim card?' he asked.

'Nah – I brought the whole phone,' I replied,

pulling it out of my pocket and putting it on the table.

'You idiot! What if he misses it?' said Dean.

'He won't. He's out cold. And he's always losing his phone anyway.'

'Let's take it to Raj at the phone shop,' said Dean. 'That way you can get it back to him and he won't suss.'

I handed him the phone.

'Check it out for yourself,' I told him, 'though the battery's a bit low.'

'No worries – I can use my charger with it if it dies,' replied Dean, reading through the messages.

'Nah – some of these texts *is* nasty . . . nah!' he said after a few minutes.

'Can Raj copy the sim card then?' I asked, not wanting to reread the messages. They had made me mad enough to begin with.

'Yeah – I rang him. He said to bring it in any-time . . .'

'So, let's go then,' I said, getting impatient.

I wanted to get it out of the way so that I could tell Dean about my new plan to get rid of Micky. The old one had been good but the new one was better and I wanted to run it by my best mate.

Dean got up and finished his juice.

'Ain't this gonna change your plan to get rid of him?' he said, putting his glass down.

'It's gonna make it easier,' I told him.

'How?'

'I'm gonna catch him, bro,' I replied.

'What, bumpin' uglies with the whale?'

I nodded.

'Rather you than me, geezer. Even thinking 'bout it is making me feel sick.'

'It's the best way,' I said. 'My other plan was too dangerous . . . this way isn't and the others don't have to get too mixed up in it.'

'True,' agreed Dean.

'I've just gotta work out how,' I told him. 'But let's go do this phone thing first.'

'Come, then,' he said. 'Let's go see the phone man, Stan . . .'

I got home an hour later, with Micky's phone and an extra sim card. Raj had transferred all the data from Micky's card over to the new one and I asked him to keep a copy on his hard drive too, just in case I lost mine. I felt a bit like a secret agent, sneaking back in quietly and replacing Micky's phone so that he wouldn't know it had been missing. I was half expecting some bald man carrying a big white cat to turn up and tell me that I was going to be killed, like in those James Bond films that I watch on telly every Christmas.

As I was putting it back, the text alert sounded and I was sure Micky would wake up, but he didn't. He stirred, mumbled something, farted twice but kept his eyes closed. The message was from his secret woman so I read it. It was a list of days and times, like a rota for lessons or work. Monday 10–3, Tuesday 9–2, Wednesday 12–2 – that sort of thing. It took me a few minutes, after I'd replaced the phone, to work out what the message meant. The woman, Tracey, was telling Micky when she was free during the week. I wondered if Micky was going to see her or if she was going to come to my mum's house. And then I realized that the latest text helped my new plan.

I grinned to myself, turning to watch Micky sleeping on the sofa. I crept over and tried a few of the beer cans. One of them was half full. I picked it up, saw his dirty, smelly trainers sitting on the floor, and tipped the lager into them. Then I placed the can so that it looked as though it had been knocked over. I didn't mind the carpet getting soaked either. It would be worth cleaning it up, especially once Micky was out of my mum's life for good.

I'd arranged to meet Suky near Grace's house, outside a bookshop called Browsers. As I was waiting I looked at my reflection in the shop window over and over again, hoping that I looked OK. I had on my one pair of smart trousers and a blue shirt, which I hadn't worn for about a year. My shoes were the same ones I wore to school but I was hoping that Suky wouldn't notice.

As I stood there, looking at myself, the lady who owned the shop smiled out at me. I looked away really quickly, feeling embarrassed. When I looked back, she was at the till wrapping a book with a bright green and orange cover for some woman. I recognized the book – it was by a local author who had gone to our school years before.

'You thinking of buying something?' I heard Suky ask me.

I turned and smiled at her. She looked really nice, all done up and that.

'Er . . . no. I ain't into books, really,' I replied.

'You should be,' she told me. 'They've got some wicked ones in there.'

'Whatever . . .'

Suky smiled and told me that we would walk back to her house.

'Cool,' I replied.

'You're not too nervous, are you?' she asked me.

I shrugged.

'It'll be fine, Jit . . . just smile and answer their questions.'

'Do I . . . er . . . do I look OK?' I asked her.

'You look fine, Jit. Don't worry about it.'

'It's just that my mum has been really busy at work and she didn't have time to wash my other clothes, and . . .'

'Jit . . . honestly, you look fine. Stop being such a worrywart about it. Relax and that way we can have a bit of fun,' Suky said.

'Fun?' I asked.

'Yeah . . . I feel quite naughty about it . . . conning my parents.'

I shook my head. 'And how you gonna feel when they catch you out?'

'They won't – stop being such a girl about it.'

'Your funeral,' I told her.

'Oh shut up!' she said with a grin.

We crossed the road, just past where Grace lives, and walked up towards Suky's house. At the first junction we went right into Dovedale. Suky's house was at the top and we walked slowly towards it, as Suky went over who was going to be at her party and apologized for her grandmother.

'I ain't even met her yet,' I said.

'Don't worry,' grinned Suky, 'you will.'

'You make her sound like a lunatic.'

'She is,' replied Suky. 'Right, this is it. You ready?'

I straightened my clothes and nodded.

'Here goes . . .' she said, leading the way.

# FOURTEEN

I walked into the hallway behind Suky, realizing for the first time just how big her house was. There were rooms off both sides of the hall and a staircase in the middle. I could hear loads of noise coming from the back of the house and every few seconds a couple of little kids ran in and out of the rooms, chasing each other.

'They're all in the dining room and kitchen,' Suky told me.

'Oh, right.'

'I'll take you in,' she said, before pausing. 'In a minute.'

'See? *You're* all worried about it now,' I said to her.

'Sshh!' she said. 'Someone will hear you.'

'Hear him say what?' came a deep voice from behind us.

I turned to see a tall Asian man standing in the

doorway, wearing a tracksuit and trainers. He was massive. I felt my stomach turn over.

'Hi, Dad!' said Suky. 'He was just talking about being nervous. Isn't that right, Imi— I mean, Jit?' she said, correcting herself quickly.

'Er . . . yeah. I was . . . feelin' all nervous an' that,' I replied, instantly wishing that I'd spoken in a posher voice.

'No need to feel nervous, son,' said Suky's dad, holding his hand out for me to shake. 'I'm Randeep.'

I took his hand and tried not to wince as he squashed it tightly in his.

'I'm Jit,' I replied.

'Jit what?'

'Huh?'

He grinned at me and put his arm around my shoulder.

'What's your surname, Jit?' he asked.

'Er . . . Kooner. Jit Kooner,' I replied, sounding like a freak.

'Well, Jit Kooner – it's good to meet you at last.'

'You too, Mr—' My mind went blank and I couldn't remember Suky's surname even though I'd seen it loads on her schoolbooks and stuff.

'Moore,' he said. 'It means "peacock" in Punjabi.'

Suky groaned.

'*What* – and *James Bond* in English?' she said to him. '*Dad* – your jokes are so lame . . .'

Her dad grinned at me like a nutter.

'And you know what "Bond" means in Punjabi, don't you?' he asked.

I grinned back. In Punjabi 'Bond' means 'arse'. I nodded.

'No need to tell you another one of me jokes then, Jit,' said her dad.

'No, there isn't, Dad,' Suky told him.

'Well best go meet the family, son,' he said. 'Mind you, some of them are a bit weird . . . but don't worry. I'll make sure you're all right.'

My stomach turned over again. Suky's dad led us into the dining room, just as someone put on a bhangra tune. I looked around and saw that the room, which was longer than my mum's entire house, was packed full of people and they all stopped to look at me. I stood where I was, frozen, wishing that I hadn't agreed to help Suky out. I was bricking myself.

'Everyone,' shouted Suky's dad. 'This is the mysterious Jit!'

Some people started whispering to each other, whilst the rest of them stood where they were, watching me. I didn't know where to look so I looked down at my feet.

'Come on, Jit,' said Suky's dad, 'let me introduce you to a few members of the family.'

I looked at Suky, who went red and walked over to a young Asian woman. It had to be her mum because they looked so alike.

'Mum, this is Jit,' she said.

Her mum smiled at me and walked over.

'Hello, Jit,' she said.

I held out my hand but she grabbed me and gave me a hug instead.

'Yeah . . . er . . . hello,' I said, wishing that she'd let me go.

'Lovely to meet you. Suky has told me all about you,' she said.

'Er, yeah. Me too,' I replied.

'She didn't tell me that you were so handsome though.'

I felt myself going red and looked down at my feet again.

'*Tina*, you've embarrassed the poor lad,' said Suky's dad.

'Oh he's OK,' replied Suky's mum. 'Aren't you, Jit?'

'Yeah – I'm fine,' I replied, wishing that someone would come and rescue me.

'Come on, Jit – let's go and talk to the men,' said Suky's dad. 'Bloody women will have you talking about clothes and make-up.'

'*Dad!*' complained Suky.

'Oh don't worry, Suky,' he replied, 'we won't keep him too long.'

He looked at me and winked.

'We're just going to have a little chat – that's all. Man to man, so to speak.'

The knot in my stomach twisted around on itself as I got ready to do a runner. I was convinced that I was going to get caught. In one of the corners, a short man in a turban made a whooping noise and turned the music up. Suddenly everyone went back to whatever they were doing, as Suky's dad told me that we were going to the conservatory.

'That's where most of the men are,' he said.

'Er . . .' I said, following him past a load of grinning women and lots of kids.

'You don't say much, do you,' he said. 'Then again

– my girl can talk for England. I bet you don't get a word in.'

I just nodded, trying to remember what Suky had said about my family. The stuff that I was supposed to remember. Suky's dad told me to sit down and introduced me to his brother, Mandeep, who was older and shorter than he was. He had really bushy eyebrows and hair coming out of his nose, and he was wearing a suit with a waistcoat. The bit of hair he had on his head was in a comb-over. He looked like a cartoon character.

'Lovely to see you, Jit,' he said, in a heavy accent.

'Er . . . yeah,' I replied for about the sixth time. I didn't know what else to say though.

I crossed my legs under the table and then uncrossed them, trying to get comfortable. Suky's dad handed me a glass of juice and sat down too, so that I was stuck between him and his brother.

'What your dad doin' then?' asked Suky's uncle.

'Er . . .'

'His surname's Kooner, Mandeep,' said Suky's dad. 'Bet we know the family.'

I gulped down a load of air.

'Kooner, eh? I think I know most of the Kooners in

the city . . . what your old man do again?' repeated the uncle.

'Owns a load of shops,' I said quickly, following Suky's story.

'Yes,' said her uncle impatiently, 'but what him sell?'

I picked up my juice and took a long drink. Long enough to try and come up with an answer. Suky hadn't told me anything about what my imaginary family did.

'Er . . . fried chicken shops,' I told them, saying the first thing that came into my head, mainly because someone had just dumped a bit plate of tandoori chicken on the table in front of us.

'*Fried chicken?*' said Suky's dad, looking puzzled.

I looked away, thinking that I'd blown it already.

'I didn't realize it was fried chicken . . .' he continued, as I waited for him to go mad and ask me who I really was.

'I thought Suky told you what his old man doing?' asked the uncle.

'Nah – she just said shops, that's all. So where are they then?' asked her dad.

I went to grab for my juice, needing to buy more time, but I didn't get hold of the glass right and I sent it flying off the table. It made a loud noise as it smashed against the white tiles on the floor.

'WHOOPS!' shouted Suky's dad.

'I'm sorry!' I said.

He gave me a funny look. 'It's only a glass, son,' he told me. 'But it must be embarrassing . . . first time round here an' all?'

I nodded. 'Yeah – I suppose it is,' I agreed, thinking that Suky's dad was a bit of a joker, and liking him for it.

'Let me get one of the kids to clean it up and get you another one,' he said.

After it had all been sorted out he asked me if I wanted a lager. I said that I didn't drink it and he looked a bit surprised. He opened a can of lager for himself and poured it into a glass.

'Well, it's here if you want it,' he told me.

I was hoping that he'd forgotten about the fried chicken shops but he was only just getting started. His brother came back over too, after getting another whisky and Coke.

'So whereabouts are they, these shops?' asked Suky's dad. 'Only you never said because you was too busy making a mess, innit?'

116

'I think they're all over the place,' I said, wishing I hadn't straight away. It was a dumb answer.

'You *think*, boy? Don't you know where your own father's shops are?' asked Suky's uncle, in Punjabi this time.

I decided to rescue the situation if I could.

'Er . . . no . . . yeah, I know where they are. They're in Birmingham and Coventry and that.'

'*Ahh!*' said her uncle. 'Because I thought it was funny. I don't know a single Punjabi chicken-shop owner in this city. They are all owned by Muslims.'

'Yeah,' agreed Suky's dad. 'And I thought I knew all the Kooners here.'

'We're *new*,' I said quickly. 'My mum wanted to move here from . . . from near Birmingham. It's nicer here.'

'But I think I know most of the Kooners in *Birmingham*, too,' said Suky's dad.

I shrugged. 'Obviously not all of them,' I said. 'You don't know my dad.'

'Might be we do,' said Uncle Mandeep. 'Whassis name then?'

'*Who?*' I asked.

'Your backside,' said Suky's uncle, being sarcastic

in Punjabi. 'Your dad – who do you think I mean?'

'Oh right, him . . . his name's Daljit,' I said, telling them the truth. My dad's name was Daljit – he just wasn't the Daljit Kooner I was telling them about.

Suky's dad nodded.

'I know a Daljit Kooner *here* but he ain't got no kids as far as I know.'

My heart nearly jumped into my mouth. What if Suky's dad knew my real dad? Only he'd said the Daljit Kooner he knew didn't have kids. So it couldn't be him.

'What about money?' asked Suky's uncle. 'How much he worth?'

I shrugged again. 'I dunno,' I told him.

'I got a great accountant if he need one. Good at hiding from the tax, innit?'

I nodded.

'So . . . how many shop he got?' Mandeep continued.

'Er . . . six,' I lied.

'Worth plenty money then!' replied Mandeep. 'He ever wanna do the business, tell him to call me. After all, we all like family now what with you seein' me niece, innit?'

'Er . . .'

'Never mind that old git,' said Suky's dad, grinning. 'He's only interested in money.'

'I don't mind—' I began.

'Yes, but Suky might. She's in there with her mum,' he said, pointing at the kitchen.

'I'll go and say hello,' I said, getting up quickly.

'Yeah, you do that,' said her old man. 'I'll be here when you're ready.'

I gave him a puzzled look. 'Ready for what?' I asked.

'To ask for my daughter, what else?' he said, getting all serious.

'I . . . er . . . I think there's been a misunder—' I stammered.

'Only kidding!' grinned Suky's dad. 'You're pretty easy to wind up, kid.'

'Yeah . . . sorry,' I said, even though I didn't have anything to apologize about.

And then, just to make things worse, I caught the edge of a mat and tripped, stumbling forward into the kitchen, straight into Suky's grandmother. '*Who's this dog?*' she shouted in Punjabi, as I tried to pretend it hadn't happened.

# FIFTEEN

I told Suky that I needed to use the loo and she showed me to one underneath the stairs. I locked myself in, put the lid down and sat, trying to calm down. I waited a few minutes and decided to wash my hands, just in case anyone was listening. The tap was one of those ones that you lift to start, only I lifted it too far, and the cold water splashed around the bowl and sprayed my shirt. I swore and looked around for tissue. I pulled a load of loo roll off and wiped myself down. Then I lifted the lid to the toilet and chucked it in, as beads of sweat started to break on my forehead. I pulled off some more loo paper and wiped my head with it.

Finally, I washed my hands and wiped them on even more loo paper. Then, I pushed the flush button. The water cascaded into the bowl and started to go round and round. But instead of the water going down into the pipes, it began to rise, slowly. I jumped back and swore again, watching the water rise, convinced

that it was going to overflow and flood the room. I
started to panic a bit, wishing that I was somewhere
else, as the water continued to rise. And then, just as it
reached the rim, it stopped. Hoping that it would
eventually disappear down the pipe, I pulled the lid
down, straightened my hair and clothes and left.

In the kitchen Suky asked me if I was OK and I
nodded, praying that no one would discover what I'd
done to the toilet.

'Mum said to give you some food,' said Suky. 'You
hungry?'

'I'm always hungry,' I said. 'What you got?'

'Usual,' she said. 'Tandoori chicken, fish, pakora,
chickpea curry and rice. Samosas too.'

I told her that chicken and samosas would be cool
and she put some onto a plate for me.

'Come on – we'll go and eat in the dining room,'
she said.

'What – with everyone else?' I said, in a panic.

'Yeah . . . why?'

'Er . . . nothing. Your granny won't be there, will
she?' I asked.

'Yeah, most probably. Don't worry – like I said,
she's nuts. No one pays her much attention,' said Suky,

trying to make me feel better.

I shrugged. 'Go on then – but how long have I got to stay?'

She shook her head.

'For a while yet. You've not been here long,' she told me.

'Yeah, but I've shown my face,' I protested.

'Come on, Jit!' she whispered angrily. 'You said you were going to help me.'

'OK, then . . . but if we get caught – you're taking all the blame,' I told her.

'Fine with me. Anyway, as long as you keep your cool – we won't get caught,' she replied.

Most of her family were eating when we went in and a couple of her aunts told me that I was a handsome boy and stuff like that. Then I sat down at the dining table, next to some kids.

'You her boyfriend?' asked a little girl with really curly hair.

'Yeah,' I said.

'EHH!' she giggled. 'He's Suky's boyfriend!'

Next to her was another girl of about the same age.

'Do you snog her?' she asked.

'You what?'

'Do you snog her?' repeated the girl.

'None of your business,' I said.

'That means you do!' said the girl, sniggering. 'That's rude!'

'Leave him alone,' said Suky, taking a seat next to me.

'So, does all your family ask rude questions?' I asked her.

'Yeah – sorry about that. They're just inquisitive – that's all,' she replied.

'Like the CIA,' I told her. 'I feel like a terror suspect.'

Suky frowned at me.

'That ain't funny,' she said.

'Yeah, I know,' I told her. 'Especially when you're the suspect.'

'Just relax, Jit. It's going fine,' she said in a whisper.

I finished my food quickly and went to get rid of my plate but her mum grabbed it from me.

'Let me get you some more, sweetheart,' she said.

'No, that's OK – I'm . . .' I began, but she ignored me and went off to the kitchen, returning with a plate load of chicken.

'Growing boy like you needs his food,' she said.

'Er . . . yeah,' I replied.

'So how did you meet Suky?' asked her mum.

'School,' I said.

'Only she didn't mention you at all until a few weeks ago,' said Suky's mum.

'Yeah – well we was . . . I mean we were all friends and then . . . well . . .'

'We just got together, sort of,' added Suky, jumping in.

'Let the boy speak, Suky,' her mum told her.

'It's OK, Mrs Moore – Suky can tell you herself. I don't mind,' I said, looking at Suky.

'It's boring anyway, Mum. It was all "my friend wants to go out with you" stuff . . . nothing too romantic.'

'Really?' replied Suky's mum. 'Shame . . .'

I shrugged and Suky's mum gave me a little smile that I couldn't work out.

'Nice food,' I said, trying to change the subject.

'Thank you, Jit,' replied her mum, grinning. 'Tell me – have you met my mother?'

'*MUM!*'

'Oh come on, Suky . . . she's a bit senile, not dangerous,' snapped her mum.

'No,' said Suky, 'she's completely off her trolley. Loopy – worse than Grace, even,' she said to me.

'That bad?' I replied, grinning.

'Well, he'll have to meet her, and I don't mean by running into her either,' said Suky's mum.

I glared at Suky.

'I didn't tell her,' complained Suky.

'No – your grandmother did,' explained her mum.

'I'm sorry about that,' I said.

'It's OK, Jit. It happens all the time,' said Suky's mum. 'But she does want to talk to you, so when you've finished, pop into the front room and say hello.'

I said that I would and returned to my extra helping of chicken.

'I think your mum's trying to fatten me up,' I told Suky, when her mum had gone.

'Yeah – she's still got that Indian thing going on – eat more, beteh,' she replied, making me laugh. Suky looked at me funny for a minute. 'You know what?' she said.

'What?' I replied.

'That's maybe the fifth time I've seen you laugh like that in all the time I've known you,' she told me.

I shrugged. 'Lucky you, then.'

'You're OK, you know that?'

I grinned. 'You ain't bad either,' I said, through a mouthful of chicken.

'Scratch that,' said Suky, looking disgusted. 'You talk with your mouth full – that's nasty!'

Suky's grandmother looked me up and down as I walked into the room at the front of the house.

'Who's this?' she asked in Punjabi.

Suky replied in Punjabi too, telling her my name.

'Jit? Jit what?'

'Kooner,' Suky told her.

She cackled to herself, showing the two teeth that she had in her mouth, and started going on about some village in the Punjab where the Kooners came from. I didn't understand all of what she said but I got most of it.

'Not as good as us,' she went on in Punjabi. 'Small village, small people . . .'

'Just ignore her,' whispered Suky, in English.

'What?' asked her gran, in Punjabi.

'Oh nothing,' I replied in Punjabi.

'Huh?'

'Sat-sri'Akaal,' I said, in Punjabi, which is how you say hello.

'You speak then, do you?' cackled Suky's gran, before giggling to herself. 'Of course, your village is full of monkeys,' she continued.

'Gran!' shouted Suky in Punjabi.

'What do you know, you ugly child?' replied Suky's gran, dissing her. 'You think I don't know that you're swearing at me in your English?'

I shook my head at Suky.

'Told you,' said Suky.

'Is a good job Imi didn't come himself,' I replied.

'Exactly . . . she would have gone mad, I reckon,' Suky told me.

'*Gone* mad?' I asked.

'OK – gone even madder than she is.'

'I dunno,' I said, 'she's quite funny in her own way.'

Just as I said that Suky's gran let rip a huge, smelly fart and then giggled to herself some more.

'Nah!!' I shouted, before laughing.

'Who you laughing at, you son of a cow-pat collector?' shouted Suky's gran in Punjabi, which just made me laugh even more.

'That's it,' said Suky. 'Let's go.'

We turned to leave and her gran dissed us some more.

'Go on – run away . . . take your son of a monkey with you, you ugly witch!'

I could still hear her cackling from the hallway. I turned to tell Suky that I wasn't bothered by what her gran had said but I didn't get the chance.

'*JIT!*' I heard her uncle shout, pronouncing my name '*Jeet*'. 'Come and tell me what your father doing. What he worth?'

I groaned.

'You got me for one more hour,' I told Suky. 'And *that's* it!'

'Thank you, thank you, thank you,' replied Suky. 'You're a star!'

'*JEEET!!!*' shouted her uncle again.

I headed back into the dining room, wondering if Suky's dad would let me have that beer now.

# SIXTEEN

I woke up on Sunday in a really good mood. I'd had fun at Suky's house in the end. It gave me an idea about what my dad's family might be like. I remembered being at family events when I was very young, but they were like dreams. Suky's party had brought it all back, though. I'd even managed to get past another meeting with her grandmother and survive. The problem came when I said I was leaving. Suky's mum said that I should come round for dinner and her dad offered to take me to watch football sometime. I'd nodded and said that I would but now we had a bigger problem. Now that we'd set up the story, we were going to have to stick to it.

And as much as I'd had a laugh at Suky's house – once was more than enough. She'd just shrugged at me and told me that she'd speak to me the following day. And I'd had to give her a kiss in front of her mum to say goodbye too, which was well weird, because I thought about Grace when I did it and felt really guilty. They'd offered me a lift home too but I said no, making up a blag about how I liked to get as much exercise as possible.

I got out of bed and had a shower before going downstairs to the zoo that was the living room. This time I didn't tidy up. Instead, I remembered my plan. I kicked a beer can out of my way and went into the kitchen, hoping to find some food. But there was nothing apart from some cold Chinese takeaway and a loaf of mouldy bread. I swore and turned back into the living room. Then I remembered that I'd nicked a tenner from Micky's jacket the day before. I smiled to myself, grabbed my coat and walked to the nearest McDonald's, where I got myself a big pile of food.

When I got back in, Micky was sitting on the sofa with a can of lager in his hands, looking rough. He gave me a stare and then went back to watching the telly. I went into the kitchen to make myself a coffee.

'Mek us one an' all,' he shouted from the living room.

I stuck my head round the door and told him to make it himself.

'You what?' he said, glaring at me.

'I said go make it yourself. I ain't your slave.'

He glared at me for a second and then he threw the beer can at me and jumped up. I stepped back into the kitchen as he approached. His face was all red and he stank of booze. He grabbed my arm and pulled me towards him.

'Who do you think you are?' he spat.

I didn't look away this time. Instead, I glared right back and told him to eff off. He gripped my arm harder and then pushed me backwards so that I stumbled and fell to the floor. He knelt over me and grabbed my ear, twisting it.

'You need to watch your mouth,' he told me. 'I'm gonna be engaged to yer mam soon and I ain't gonna tek no crap from you, unnerstand?'

I nodded, hoping that he would let go of my ear, which was burning with pain.

'GOOD!' he spat, kicking me in the thigh. 'Now mek me a coffee – there's a good boy . . .'

An hour later, I still hadn't seen my mum. I walked over to Grace's house, angry and scared, but determined too. Her mum answered, telling me to come in out of the cold. 'It's freezing out there, Jit,' she said to me. 'And you've not even got a jacket on!'

'I forgot to put it on, Mrs Parkhurst,' I lied.

I hadn't even noticed the cold until she mentioned it. Looking down at my hands, I saw that they were red and frozen.

'Are you OK, Jit?' she asked, looking concerned. 'You look like you've been crying.'

'I'm fine – honestly. It's just a bit windy, that's all, and it makes my eyes water.'

Grace's mum was about to say something else when she saw the look on my face and stopped herself.

'Go on downstairs,' she said. 'I'll get Madam for you. And if there's anything you ever want to talk about, Jit, just ask me – OK?'

I nodded.

'OK?' she repeated.

'Yes – thanks, Mrs Parkhurst,' I mumbled.

Grace joined me in her cellar about five minutes later. I'd been knocking a few balls around on the pool table and trying to calm down. I didn't even know what I was going to say to her. I just had it in my head that I needed to tell her what was going on. Not just the plan to get rid of Micky but everything else as well. And that was making me edgy.

'What's up?' asked Grace, as soon as she saw my face. I shrugged.

'And this time – don't lie about it. I want to know,' she told me.

She walked over to me and put her arms out to give me a hug. I waited for a few seconds, hugged her back and then, even though I didn't want to, and it made me feel like a kid, I started to cry.

I told her everything. Not just the stuff about the plan but all of it, right from when I was little. All the stuff about my dad leaving us, which my mum had told me, through to Micky turning up, the drinking, the lot. And when I'd finished, I made Grace promise not to tell anyone unless I asked her to. She just sat and looked at me, all sad and upset.

'Why didn't you just tell someone?' she asked me. 'The teachers at school or my parents? Just some-one . . .'

I shrugged again.

'All those times that you got into trouble and just walked out of lessons – we thought you were just being rebellious. Hannah told me that you'd been like that since you were little,' she said.

'I know,' I replied.

'We could tell my parents now,' she said.

'No!'

'But, Jit . . .'

'I don't want you to. You promised . . . and anyway, I've got a plan to get rid of him now.'

'What's that?'

'I'm gonna catch him with the other woman – get evidence. That's what I need to speak to Imi and Suky about. I need to borrow a camera.'

Grace looked up and half smiled.

'Let me ask my dad,' she said.

She went upstairs and for a moment I thought that she would tell him everything. I started to panic but then I stopped. Inside I knew that she wouldn't say anything. I was just being paranoid. She came back down a few minutes later and shook her head.

'It's at his partner's office,' she told me. 'They're using it all week – sorry.'

'No worries,' I told her. 'Imi said he'd got one so I'm gonna ask for that.'

Grace raised her eyebrows.

'Will he do that – lend it to you, I mean?'

I grinned, feeling much better than I had done in ages.

'After what I went through last night at Suky's?' I replied. 'You better believe it, Sister Gee.'

Grace smiled wide at that.

'Ooh – call me that again,' she said. 'In a French accent, this time.'

'Huh?'

'Only kidding,' she said, leaning over and giving me a kiss on the cheek.

'What was that for?' I asked.

'Just because . . .' she replied. 'Now let's call the lovers, tell them to get their stinky bums over here, and I'll kick your fat ass at pool whilst we're waiting.'

'You can try,' I said, grinning even wider.

Imi was funny about lending me his brand-new camera until Suky said that they owed me a favour. He nodded and handed it to me, telling me to be careful with it.

'No problem, bro,' I told him.

'It cost over three hundred quid,' Imi told me.

'Yeah – I said I wouldn't break it or nothing,' I replied.

'You better not.'

I thanked him and told them some of the stuff

about Micky. Not everything that I'd told Grace but all the important bits. Suky shook her head when I'd finished and held my hand.

'That's horrible,' she said, only I wasn't looking at her. I was too busy watching Grace, who looked surprised or angry or something. I couldn't work it out.

'No need to steal his hand, is there?' Grace said to Suky.

Suky looked at her like she was mad. 'What?' she asked.

'You *can* let go of him,' repeated Grace.

Suky grinned.

'Me thinks someone's jealous,' she joked.

'No, I'm not . . . you're just smothering him, that's all!' replied Grace.

'Oh grow up!' said Suky.

'Smelly gimp!' said Grace, only now she was smiling.

'Moo!'

'Witch!'

I shook my head.

'Leave it out,' I told them.

They looked at each other and started giggling.

'Shut up, you weirdo!' they replied together, like they were twins or something.

I looked to Imi for support but he had a serious look on his face.

'You sure about this plan?' he asked.

'Yeah – why?'

'I just don't get why you can't tell your mum, show them text messages . . .'

'She's thrown him out three times before but she always takes him back,' I told him. 'It's like she's blind to what he does and that.'

'Yeah, but—' began Imi.

'Yeah, but nuttin'. She needs to have the evidence right there in her face,' I said. 'It's the only way she'll really believe it.'

'If you say so,' replied Imi, ''cos you'll get into trouble at school.'

'I'm already in trouble,' I told him, remembering that I was going to have to face Mr Singh the next morning. 'What's a bit more trouble gonna do?'

Imi shrugged and told me that I was mad.

'Maybe,' I told him.

Maybe I was – but I didn't care. Micky was on his way out of my mum's life, whether he liked it or not. That was just the way things were going to be.

# SEVENTEEN

Mrs Dooher waited until she'd finished reading out the messages to speak to me. I had made an effort to get to school early, just to try and get in her good books but it didn't work.

'Jit – can I see you out in the corridor for a minute?' she asked.

'*Eh! Jit's in trouble!*' shouted Marco, one of my class.

'Gonna get his ass whipped, innit, miss?' said Dilip.

'Mind your own business,' replied Mrs Dooher.

'But he's gonna get it, ain't he?' said Marco's twin brother, Milorad.

'*Isn't* he . . .' corrected Mrs Dooher.

'Still gonna get it,' shouted Milorad.

I stood up and gave the twins a death stare. They looked away. Dean stood up too, went over to Dilip and the other lads and whispered.

'Careful,' he told them.

'But—' began Dilip.

'*But, miss, I'm picking my teeth up off the floor,*' said Dean, in a high-pitched voice.

Dilip went red and shut up.

'Anyone *else* got summat they wanna say?' asked Dean, looking really angry.

No one replied. Mrs Dooher looked at me and shook her head.

'Come on,' she said softly.

Out in the corridor she told me what was going on.

'Mr Singh has spoken to Mrs Orton about Geography,' she said.

'What – so I'm gonna have to spend the *whole* first lesson with Singh?'

'*Mr* Singh, Jit, and yes you are,' she replied.

'But . . .'

'It's too late for that,' she told me.

'What's gonna happen?' I asked.

'We have to report all unscheduled absences, Jit. Your mum should have spoken to Mr Singh last week. Now that she hasn't – we're forced to take other measures.'

'I'm sorry,' I said, trying to get out of it.

She shook her head.

'Maybe you are but that's beside the point, I'm

afraid. We don't want to do this, Jit, but we don't make the rules any more.'

I looked down at my feet and tried to think of a way out. Just a small blag to cover my tracks until I could sort out Micky.

'OK,' I said. 'You want me to go see him *now*?'

'No, you can go after registration finishes,' she told me.

I nodded.

'And, *Jit*?'

'Yeah?'

'If there's *anything* going on – anything at all – with home or whatever – now is the best time to tell us.'

I shrugged.

'OK – get back inside,' she said.

'Thanks, miss.'

I went back into class and sat down next to Hannah and Grace.

'You *all right*?' asked Grace.

I shook my head.

'What's up?' asked Hannah.

'I think they're about to throw me out,' I told them.

'*Really?*' asked Grace, looking worried.

I shrugged. 'Ain't sure, but miss was talking about

taking other measures and stuff,' I told them.

'They have to exclude you temporarily first, don't they?' asked Hannah.

'I dunno.'

'What are we gonna do?' asked Grace, making me smile a bit because she'd said 'we' and not 'you'.

'I need a story,' I told her. 'Just to cover me until I can catch Micky.'

'Er . . .' began Grace.

'Your mum's really ill though, *isn't* she?' said Hannah, winking.

'Huh?'

'Your *mum*. She works with mine, doesn't she? And *my* mum told me that *your* mum is off work this week,' she continued, winking about four times.

I started to get what she was doing.

'*Yeah* . . . and I need to get home at lunch time to go *check* on her but I'll be back for the afternoon and that . . .' I said, playing along.

Hannah nodded.

'And I'll *have* to back up any story you tell miss, or Mr Singh, obviously,' she added.

'*Obviously*,' grinned Grace.

'Right – just act sad,' said Hannah, to both of us.

'*What* you on about?' asked Dean.

'*Just act sad*,' repeated Hannah, 'and tell the lovers to do the same.'

Dean leaned over and whispered to Imi and Suky. Imi tried to complain but Dean said something else to him and he started nodding. He looked at me and winked. I looked up at Mrs Dooher, feeling bad about blagging her, but I didn't really have a choice.

'*Miss?*' I said.

'Yes, Jit?' she asked.

'I think there's something you need to know.'

She told me to follow her into the corridor again. Once we were out of the room, I put on a really sad face. Not that I needed to think about it, I was good at being sad for real.

'You know you asked me to tell you summat . . . if there was summat wrong and that?' I said.

'Yes, and I meant it too,' replied Mrs Dooher.

'Well . . . er . . . it's my mum,' I told her.

'Your *mum?*'

'Yeah – she's really, really ill and I don't know what to do and things ain't been right and . . .'

Mr Singh looked from me to Grace to Hannah in

his office about twenty minutes later.

'And this is the *truth*, right?' he asked us. 'Only you could find yourselves in serious trouble if you're lying. *Serious* trouble.'

'It is the truth,' insisted Hannah. 'Why would my mum tell me lies?'

'Right,' said Mr Singh. 'So what is it you need from me, Jit?'

'Just a few days to get my mum in to see you,' I told him.

'And you need to go home for lunch times?' he added.

'Yeah – but I'll be back for lessons.'

He nodded.

'Your lunch times are your own, anyway,' he said to me.

'I know that . . . I just don't want you thinking that I've done a bunk. I thought it would be better to tell you what's happening.'

'Well, yes it would,' said Mr Singh.

'So I am.'

'And it took two of your friends to tell me too?' he asked.

'Would you have believed me otherwise?' I said.

'OK – that's fine but you still aren't out of

trouble, Jit. As long as you understand.'

'Yeah – I do,' I replied.

'And one more thing, Jit.'

I looked at Grace and Hannah, wondering what it was. Mr Singh started to type something out on his computer.

'I need you to get your mum to sign this for me, today, when you go home for lunch. If I *don't* get this from you straight after lunch – the deal's off. Do you understand?'

He hit the print button.

'Yeah.'

'Right – get to your lessons and remember – if you're lying to me, I *will* find out.'

All three of us nodded and left his office. In the corridor, Grace and Hannah asked me if I was sure about what I was doing.

'Yeah – I'm sure. I've gotta be anyhow,' I told them.

'Why's that?' asked Hannah.

''Cos if I mess up now – you two are gonna get into serious trouble and I'm gonna get thrown out of school,' I said quietly.

We walked back to our Geography lesson without saying another word.

# EIGHTEEN

At lunch time I ran out of school and down to the bus stop. The board above the shelter said that the next bus was due in two minutes and the entire journey would take me another fifteen. I didn't have much time to spare. When the bus arrived, I got on and sat downstairs, so that I wouldn't have too far to move when I needed to get off. As each stop went by I got more and more nervous about what I was about to do. What if Micky caught me? What if I was wrong and the other woman wasn't going to be at my mum's house? As I sat and thought about it, I pulled out the note that Mr Singh had printed off, got out my pen and forged my mum's signature. It wasn't like I hadn't done it before. And at least this time there was a real reason to do it. A proper excuse.

The bus eventually pulled up at my stop and I ran off up the main road. As I turned into my road I bumped straight into Gussie, Dean's older brother.

'Easy, my yout' – where's the fire?' he asked me.

'Sorry, Gussie . . . I've just gotta get home quick.'

Dean's brother grinned at me.

'You ain't gonna make it home if you don't watch where you're goin',' he told me.

'OK,' I said, hoping that he wouldn't ask me anything else.

'So, why you gotta go home anyway?' he said.

'Er . . . just gotta grab summat . . . need it for school,' I mumbled.

'And how's them games selling – the ones I gave Dean?' he continued.

'Cool – look I gotta run, bro. Can I chat to you later?' I asked.

Gussie shrugged. 'I was only askin',' he said.

I didn't hear what else he said because I looked up and saw Micky and a woman getting out of a battered old car, about a hundred metres up the street. I ducked behind a parked car.

'What the raas—!?' Gussie began, but I grabbed him before he could finish and pulled him down to where I was hiding.

'*SSHH!*'

He looked at me like I was mad and then peered

round the corner to see what I was looking at.

'Ain't that your mum's house they're goin' into?' he whispered.

'Yeah ... er ... I'll tell you in a minute ...' I told him.

Micky was fishing in his pocket for something, and the woman, who had that fake blonde hair and was wearing a short skirt that was way too small, grabbed him from behind. He turned, holding the keys, smiled and snogged her.

'Nah ... that's *nasty*,' whispered Gussie. 'That woman belongs on one a dem TV show, man ... Obese Britain or some ting!'

'*SSHH!*' I said again.

I watched them go into my mum's house and shut the door behind them. Then I stood up. Gussie did the same.

'Right ... you gonna tell me what's goin' on?' he said.

'Er ...'

'Who's the geezer?'

'That's Micky ... me mum's boyfriend.'

Gussie looked shocked. 'An' he's kissin' up that bog beast pon the street like *that*?'

'Yeah . . . I'm trying to catch him out,' I said.

'You done catch him then,' Gussie replied. 'What you gonna do now?'

'Go back to school,' I said.

Gussie gave me a funny look before grinning.

'Tell you what,' he said, 'I'll do yer a deal. I'll ring me mate, Reedy, and get him to drop you off at school, *if*, on the way, you tell me what the *raas* is goin' on!'

I looked at Gussie and shrugged. Getting a lift back to school would mean that I'd definitely be on time. I nodded, wondering if Gussie would be useful to my plan.

'Yeah, thanks,' I replied. 'Maybe you can help me out too?'

'You want me to kick his ass?' asked Gussie.

'Nah – not just yet. It's summat else.'

Gussie grinned. 'Well you better tell me after I ring Reedy and get him to pick us up,' he replied.

'Won't take long, will it? Only I gotta be back on time or I'm dead,' I asked.

'Soon come,' he told me. 'Nuh worry yuhself, bro . . .'

Back at school, my mind was racing. I couldn't sit still

in Mr Wilson's Science lesson and twice he told me to stop fidgeting. Dean, Grace and the others wanted to know what was going on but I couldn't tell them until afternoon break. When we did get together, out by the tennis courts, they were more nervous than I was.

'What?' asked Dean, impatiently.

'Yeah . . . tell us what happened,' added Hannah.

I grinned at them. 'We caught him . . . me and Gussie,' I said.

'*Gussie?*' said Dean in surprise.

'Dean's brother?' added Imi.

'Yep – I bumped into him on my street and we saw them.'

'What's she like?' asked Grace. 'Is she ugly?'

'Seriously rank,' I told her.

'One of them that when they're born, the midwife slaps the mother?' asked Dean.

'Exactly,' I replied.

'URGH!' said Suky.

'Yeah,' I said. 'Anyway, I told Gussie all about it on the way back to school.'

'Gussie came to school?' asked Dean, looking worried.

'Nah – he got his mate, Reedy, to give me a lift.'
Dean nodded.

'Anyway,' I continued.

'Yeah – let him get a word in,' interrupted Grace.

'*Anyway*,' I said again, 'I told Gussie, and him and Reedy are gonna help out with the plan.'

'Huh?' asked Imi.

'Don't worry,' I told them. 'The plan's only changed a little bit. But we're gonna do it on Wednesday.'

'*This* Wednesday?' asked Grace.

'Yep . . . I was right about those times in her text.'

'Texts – what texts?' asked Imi.

I told him it didn't matter what texts.

'Let's just get together tonight and sort it out,' I said.

'At my house!' said Grace, excited.

'Yeah . . . Everyone OK with that?'

They all nodded.

# NINETEEN

'OWW!'

I gave Dean a dirty look.

'He's standin' on my foot,' he explained.

'Shut up – they'll hear us!' I told him.

Gussie and his friend Reedy were standing right behind us, in the back yard of my mum's house. It was Reedy who'd stood on Dean's foot. And he was about eighteen stone.

We were waiting for Imi and Suky to play their part in my plan, by knocking on the front door. But that wasn't for another five minutes. I pointed at the lock on my mum's back door.

'I checked it,' I told Reedy. 'It's a Yale one.'

'Cool,' he replied, pulling out two credit-card-sized pieces of plastic.

'You sure you can get us in?' I asked.

'Easy,' whispered Reedy.

I moved out of the way and he stood in front of the

back door. He took one card and wedged it between the door and the frame, under the lock. The other one went above it. Then he started to wiggle the cards about, trying to push them through. He was pushing them really hard and his face went red. I looked at Dean, who was frowning.

'What?' I whispered.

He pointed back at Reedy. When I looked, I saw what he was disgusted at. Reedy's jeans had fallen and his bum crack was showing. I looked back at Dean and shook my head.

'Nasty!' I said.

'You're telling me,' he replied.

'Hurry up nuh, man!' Gussie told Reedy.

'I'm goin' as fast as I can,' Reedy replied.

Suddenly, there was a popping sound and the back door was open.

'Is it that easy?' asked Dean.

'Told yer,' said Reedy.

'Bro – you ain't never comin' round my house again,' Gussie told him.

'Get lost,' replied Reedy. 'I ain't no thief! My dad is a locksmith and I used to help him and that.'

I told them to shut up as I crept slowly into the

kitchen, praying that Micky was upstairs with his bog beast. The door into the living room was shut, so I told the lads to come in. Then I shut the door as quietly as I could.

'What now?' asked Dean.

'Now we give the other two the signal,' I said.

Dean pulled out his mobile and called Imi, letting it ring three times before hanging up.

'You ready?' I asked them, pulling out the camera that Imi had lent me.

They nodded.

'Cool . . .'

My stomach was turning over and over as I waited for the doorbell to go. I was having last-minute jitters but it was too late for those. The plan was up and running and nothing was gonna stop it now. It took about two minutes and then the doorbell started ring-ing. I listened out for movement from upstairs. Nothing happened.

The doorbell stopped ringing for about ten seconds and then it started again. This time I heard something: banging doors, heavy steps and then another door, the one at the bottom of the stairs into the living room. It was Micky. I could hear him swearing.

'Ready?' I whispered, grabbing the kitchen door.

They nodded. I waited until I heard the front door open.

'One, two . . . THREE!' I shouted and we ran into the living room.

Gussie and his mate ran to the front door, just as Micky was turning round to see what the noise was all about. The shock on his face when he saw two big lads charging at him would have been mild compared to how he felt when they shoulder-barged him out of the house and shut the door on him.

I grabbed Dean and ran up the stairs, taking them two by two. At the top I turned into my mum's room and saw the bog beast lying on the bed, naked. I felt the urge to throw up but I didn't have time. She screamed as I grabbed the camera and started taking photos. Dean told her not to move. The woman – Tracey, I guess – swore at us and tried to cover herself up with the covers. But I already had my evidence and I told Dean that we were going.

My plan then was to go downstairs, face Micky, show him the pictures and tell him that he had to leave or I'd show them to my mum. It didn't go that way though. When I got to the front door, it was open and

Gussie and Micky were scuffling in the street. Micky had answered the door wearing my mum's dressing gown and Gussie had ripped it open. Micky only had on his boxer shorts underneath and everyone in the street was watching the scuffle.

I told them to stop.

'He called me a monkey . . .' said Gussie.

'You are a monkey, you black—' began Micky, only he didn't finish.

Instead, he realized that he wasn't fighting with a burglar because I was there, holding a camera and grinning.

'What the hell do you think you're doin'?' he shouted, all red in the face.

I held up the camera. Behind him I could see Imi and Suky watching.

'I got your girlfriend on camera,' I told him.

'You sly, conniving likkle . . .'

'You got a choice,' I told him. 'Either you leave right now and take the troll with you, or I'm gonna show these to Mum and you'll get kicked out anyway.' I heard a car screeching up behind us in the street. Probably more spectators.

Then Micky went for me. I managed to throw

Dean the camera, just before he reached me, his fist catching me right on the nose. We fell to the floor and I was trying to hit and kick him but my head felt like someone was poking hot needles into it and I was in tears. The robe had come off completely now and Micky was going mad. I could hear other people shouting too. I closed my eyes.

The next thing I knew, Micky had been pulled off me. I opened my eyes and saw Mr Singh and Mr Black holding Micky, who tried to punch them too. I saw Mr Singh land a counter punch in Micky's ribs. And then Micky was on the ground, in just his boxer shorts, coughing. I got up, holding my nose, and saw Grace and Hannah. I couldn't work out why they were there. They were supposed to have been at school, to cover for the rest of us. Had they told Mr Singh everything? Is that why Singh and Black had turned up?

And then I saw that there was someone else with them. It was my mum and she was crying . . .

# TWENTY

It took about a week for everything to calm down again. Micky moved out of our house the same day, along with his other woman, in her battered old car, with my mum going mad at him and threatening to kill him if he ever came back. She didn't mean it, but Micky didn't know that and he looked genuinely scared when she went for him. Mr Singh had to hold her back. Then she went inside and started crying loads. When I joined her, she wouldn't stop saying sorry. In the end, I had to shout at her to tell her that I was OK and that I didn't blame her for Micky. And since then things have been brilliant. She's even cut down on her drinking, which is a start, I suppose.

As for school, Mr Singh got us all together a few days later, along with Mr Black, and they made us tell them everything that had happened. And I mean, everything, right down to the lies that we had told. I told the teachers that it was all my fault. I'd made my mates get involved and I'd made them lie for me. Mr Singh listened as I was talking but said that he was still going to punish the others. It wasn't like they were going to be excluded or anything though. Then he told them to leave us alone.

They filed out slowly, as I waited to see what would happen. Once they'd gone, Mr Black spoke first.

'You know, Jit, you've been a pain in my backside ever since you came to Devana High.'

'Yessir,' I mumbled.

'You've lied, cheated, fought, played truant, encouraged your friends to get into trouble and generally been a nuisance all round,' he continued.

I shrugged. I could see what was coming.

'But then you decide that our warnings aren't sufficient and that you're going to break the school rules whenever you choose to. This is not on, as I'm sure you're aware . . .'

He held up a brown envelope, as Mr Singh walked back into the room. I looked at him, hoping for some support, but he looked away.

'So, the question is . . . What do we do with you? The obvious answer, I'm afraid, is exclusion for a month, followed by a meeting between ourselves, your mother, the governors and social services.'

'BUT!' I shouted.

'Now, now, Jit, do let me finish . . . I may be firm but I'm fair with it,' said Mr Black.

'But you can't throw me out . . . I was just trying to . . .' I began, only I didn't finish.

'This is a letter that we typed last Friday, Jit, to inform you and your mother that we were about to exclude you for a month, pending further action. It's the last door before the one marked exit, and you, young sir . . .'

I gulped down air, feeling sick. It was gonna happen. I was about to get kicked out of school. I thought about my friends. Dean and Hannah and the lovers. And I thought about Grace. I could feel the tears beginning to well up inside me, along with the anger. My brain was going haywire.

'. . . Have managed, with an act of extreme stupidity, it must be said, to pull yourself back from the brink.'

I blinked through the tears and thought about what Mr Black had just said. I'd thought that he was going to throw me out, but it sounded like . . .

'. . . And considering the circumstances in which

you've found yourself for the last eighteen months, I've decided to offer you a reprieve.'

I looked at Mr Singh, who grinned at me. Then I looked at Mr Black, who smiled and then tore the letter up.

'But—' I began.

'No "buts", Jit. You're being given two days' leave of absence from school to sort out things at home. I've spoken to your mother and she is very happy for you to have the time off. Mr Singh will see you home.'

I looked at them both and tried to blink back more tears but I couldn't. I didn't know what to say or what to do. Everything was going fine, which was new to me, and I didn't know how to deal with it.

'Thank you,' I managed to say.

Mr Black shook his head.

'No need for thanks, son. Firm but fair, that's all. Firm but fair. Now, go away before I change my mind . . .'

# SUKY

# ONE

'Suky!'

I opened my bedroom door and called down to my mum. 'I'm up!'

'Well come downstairs then,' she replied.

I checked my hair in the mirror one more time, grabbed my school bag and went downstairs to the kitchen, where my mum and dad were eating toast. My dad wiped crumbs from his mouth before speaking to me, the dirty old git.

'You want a lift?' he said.

I grabbed a slice of toast as I replied, 'Please.'

My dad grinned. I knew there was something else coming. Something that only he would think was funny.

'Want to pick up the boyfriend on the way?' he teased.

'Er . . . no – he makes his own way to school,' I told him.

I was talking about *both* of my boyfriends. My real one, Imtiaz, and my fake one, Jit. My parents had only met Jit and that was who my dad was on about. I put some jam on my toast and started to eat, hoping that my dad would lay off. As I finished it, my grandma walked into the kitchen, holding her false teeth.

'Aren't you going to get dressed?' she mumbled in Punjabi, looking at me.

'I'm *already* dressed,' I pointed out.

'Stupid cow,' replied my grandma.

I suppose I should explain a few things really. First off, my grandma is completely senile so no one batted an eyelid when she called me a stupid cow. Secondly, there's a good reason why I've got 'two' boyfriends. My real boyfriend is called Imtiaz. He's in my class at school and I've known him since infant school. But he's Muslim and my parents are Sikhs, and I thought they might have a problem with him even though they know Imi – they've met him and his parents loads of times. My parents started asking me to bring my boyfriend home so that they could meet him and I kind of lied and told them I was seeing a lad called Jit, who is Sikh, and in my class at school. They met Jit and liked him and now I'm stuck. It's a delicate situation and one of these days I'm going to have to tell them the truth, but not yet.

My dad, whose name is Randeep, zipped his tracksuit top over his beer belly and told me to hurry up.

'I'm ready,' I replied.

'And, by the way,' added my mum, who's called Tina, 'we're planning a family day trip to the seaside soon. You can ask Jit along if you like.'

I swallowed hard. Would Jit go for that? He'd already helped me out enough, coming along to various family events, only to get a grilling from my Uncle Mandeep and my dad; and to get sworn at by the mad witch who was masquerading as my grandmother.

'Er . . . I'll see what he says,' I replied.

My grandma farted.

'That son of a *dung* collector?' she said, to no one in particular. 'Tell him we don't want his kind in this house. He's so ugly I cry every time I see him.'

I gave her a dirty look before getting up from the table.

'Just ignore her,' my mum advised.

'Have you cleaned your teeth, you witch?' added my gran, looking at my mum.

My dad shook his head and started giggling like a little boy.

'Don't encourage her,' my mum hissed.

'She don't need any encouragement,' he replied. 'Mad as a pregnant water buffalo, that one.'

I grinned at my dad.

'Come on then,' he said. 'Let's get you to school so that you can play kissing games with Jit.'

'Dad!'

My school is called Devana High, which is a stupid name for a school if you ask me, but it's kind of a cool place. The principal, Mr Black, was standing at the school gates as usual, watching the pupils arrive.

'Early again, Miss Kaur,' he bellowed at me in his foghorn voice.

'Yessir,' I mumbled, hoping that he'd leave me alone.

'We should present you with an award for your timekeeping,' he added, beaming a wide smile in my direction, just as another of my classmates, Hannah, turned up.

'Er . . . yes, sir,' I said, feeling embarrassed.

'Ooh nerdy bum lick,' whispered Hannah, before giggling.

'Shut up,' I told her, as we walked into school through the main entrance.

'Well – you and your nice relationship with Black – you're a creep!'

'But you're always on time too,' I reminded her, 'so what does that make you?'

'Diligent and punctual,' she replied. 'But neither of those things involves being a bum lick.'

'Oh, get lost.'

We walked into our form room and took our usual seats. Imtiaz (my *real* boyfriend) was already there and he smiled at me as I sat down.

'Hi,' I said.

'You all right?' he asked me.

'Yeah – why wouldn't I be?' I replied.

'It's just that you said you were going to call me yesterday and you didn't,' he told me, looking like a little boy.

'Sorry . . . forgot,' I replied, feeling a bit guilty.

'How can you *forget* to call your boyfriend?' asked Hannah, before grinning. 'Oh *yeah* – you've got *two* . . .'

I looked at Imi, whose face fell.

'I've only got one *real* boyfriend,' I corrected. 'Jit's just like a stand-in.'

'You spend enough time with him, though,' added Hannah.

I glared at her. Didn't she get it? I didn't want her to wind up Imi by talking about Jit. Talk about upsetting the applecart. I think she got my meaning because she went red.

'So, you just forgot?' continued Imi.

'Er . . . yeah. I was with my mum and dad and didn't get a chance and . . .'

'It doesn't matter,' he added.

I grinned at him. Behind us our form tutor, Mrs Dooher, walked in.

'Morning!' she said in her lovely Liverpudlian accent.

'Hi, miss!' beamed Hannah.

'And you call *me* a bum lick?' I said.

'Oh shut up – Mrs Dooher is lovely.'

'So is Mr Black,' I pointed out.

'Is what, Suky?' asked Mrs Dooher from behind me.

'A nice man,' I said quickly.

'And you're talking about him because . . .?' she continued.

'We're just comparing teachers, miss,' said Hannah, winking at me. 'You know – who we really like and who we don't. You came top of the list!'

Mrs Dooher smiled warily.

'Soft gits . . .' she said, before turning her attention to Marco and Milorad, twin brothers who were having a scuffle.

'STOP IT!' she half shouted.

'But he called me a toad licker!' squealed Marco.

'Didn't!' replied his twin brother.

'Why a toad licker?' asked Mrs Dooher, as Jit, Dean and Grace walked in, two minutes before time.

'Who's lickin' toads, miss?' asked Dean.

'No one,' I told him. 'The ugly twins are having a scrap, that's all.'

'Who you callin' ugly?' shouted Marco. 'Have you seen a mirror lately?'

I felt myself go red, but Jit stepped in.

'You'll be ugly when I've finished with you,' he told Marco.

'Uglier than your brother,' added Dean, 'and my guy is butt ugly, you get me? I seen better-looking warts than him.'

Mrs Dooher sighed and told us all to sit down.

'But why a toad licker?' asked Grace. 'That's just dirty.'

'You *can* lick toads though,' said Dean.

'HUH?' asked Hannah.

'Yeah – they got 'em in South America. They lick them and get all high and that – except for one yellow one though. If you licked *that* toad you'd be dead!'

'But why would anyone *want* to lick a toad – stinky, smelly . . .' continued Grace, only I switched off because Jit asked me if I was OK.

'Yes – how about you?'

'All right,' he told me. 'Them twins won't be picking on you again.'

I gave him a big smile; only Imi saw me do it and I could tell by the look on his face that he was throwing a wobbly. So I gave *him* an even bigger smile but it was too late. Imi looked away and started talking to a lad called Dilip instead.

# TWO

I wanted to ask Jit about my family trip to the seaside although I couldn't be sure that he would agree to come along. He'd already been to a few family events, and our 'little blag', as he called it, wasn't supposed to have been a long-term thing. I was *supposed* to find a way of telling my parents about Imi gently – you know, test the water first – but it was just too easy to pretend that Jit was my boyfriend. Plus, I had cold feet about telling my parents the truth anyway, so I was happy for things to continue as they were. Only there was Grace too, who pretended that she didn't fancy Jit but had been funny with us both since our 'blag' had begun.

I was walking into English with Hannah, Imi and Grace when I saw Jit. Imi saw him too and when I took Jit to one side, Imi frowned at me. I waited for him to go into the classroom before I spoke. I could always talk him round later.

'I need another favour,' I blurted out.

Jit shrugged.

'What this time?' he asked.

'Family day out . . . to the seaside,' I told him.

'*Suky* . . .'

'I know I said the other week would be the last time but my dad just dropped this on me.'

'I dunno,' he told me. 'We're gonna get caught out one day . . . why don't you just tell your dad the truth?'

I shrugged.

'I'm going to – soon, I promise. It's just that he really likes you and . . .'

'But that just makes it worse,' he told me. 'The more he thinks that you an' me are seein' each other – the harder it's going to be to tell him about Imi.'

'Just one more time . . . please?' I begged.

'I dunno, Suky. I'm not into all this jugglin' business.'

'Jugglin'?'

'Yeah – you know. Like the way you're jugglin' two lads an' that.'

'Oh right . . . *Jugglin'* – I like it . . . so will you think about it at least?' I asked.

'Yeah, OK. But I'm not sitting in a car with your

gran – she called me a one-legged son of a vulture the other week.'

'I thought that you couldn't speak Punjabi that well?' I said, grinning.

'I can't – your old man told me what she was on about and then he laughed at me for ages.'

'I'm *sorry*,' I said, in a girly voice, feeling a bit guilty because it was the voice I used when I was flirting with Imi.

'I'll tell you whether I can help later,' Jit said.

'GET INTO THE CLASSROOM!' shouted our English teacher, Mr Herbert.

'Yeah, yeah,' sighed Jit, walking over to Dean and sitting down. I walked past them and sat down by Imi. Dilip and another boy, Mohammed, whistled as I took my chair.

'QUIET!' squawked Herbert, going red in the face.

'Kiss my fat raas,' muttered Dean.

Herbert's head snapped round so fast that I thought it would come off.

'WHAT DID YOU SAY?' he demanded.

Dean grinned. 'I said that school discipline is a farce,' he lied. 'A big *fat* farce . . .'

'Well keep it to yourself,' warned Herbert.

'If I was as ugly as you, I would,' muttered Jit.

'WHAT?'

'I *said* that it doesn't take much to be good,' lied Jit. 'In school, I mean . . .'

'And you're the expert, are you?' sneered Herbert. The red mark on his forehead, where he'd squeezed a giant pimple a few weeks earlier, turned a darker shade. I smiled at the memory of seeing him walk back into the room with a load of blood where his spot used to be. It had been one of the funniest things that I had ever seen.

At lunch time I was sitting in a classroom with Hannah and Grace, working on the school newspaper, when Imi walked in looking like someone had slapped his face with a dead fish.

'What's up with you?' asked Grace. 'You look ill.'

'Nothing,' he replied, pulling up a chair. 'What you doin'?'

I showed him some magazine articles on chat-up lines.

'We're doing a feature on rubbish boys and what they say to try and pull girls,' Hannah told him.

'Yeah – like "Did you fall out of Heaven . . . ?" and other silly stuff,' added Grace.

'Oh,' replied Imi.

'What's up?' This time I was asking.

Imi shrugged. 'Just feeling a bit under the weather,' he told me.

He was lying. I knew what was up with him, and I told him that we needed to talk. Hannah and Grace both raised their eyebrows, like they were twins. I scowled at them and walked into the corridor, behind Imi. I didn't say anything until the door was firmly closed and the twins couldn't hear what we were saying.

'It's about Jit, isn't it?' I said to Imi.

'NO!'

'Yes, it is.'

He shrugged.

'You just seem to be spending a load of time with him,' he said. 'You may as well be going out with him.'

'But I'm not,' I told him. 'I'm going out with you!'

'Yeah . . .'

'Yeah – nothing. All this stuff with Jit is just to fool my parents. It's not *real*.'

'May as well be *real*,' he sulked.

'*Imi!*'

'He was even standing up for you this morning with Marco. He's never done that before.'

'Yes he has – and anyway we're much better friends than we used to be. He's cool.'

Imi looked down at his feet as I realized my mistake. I'd put my foot in it.

'Oh, you *know* what I mean,' I insisted. 'I'm just jugglin' – that's all. Not because I want to but—'

'*See?* You're even beginning to talk like him. Since when did you use words like *that?*'

'Like what?'

'Jugglin' . . . what's that all about?'

I shook my head. Imi was beginning to wind me up. I really liked him, and I could understand why he was bothered, but there was a limit.

'It's only a *word*,' I said.

'No – it's a *Jit* word,' he replied. Then he walked off.

'*IMI!*' I shouted after him but he didn't reply.

I swore under my breath and went back into the classroom, pushing the door open to find Grace and Hannah behind it.

'Oh, great!' I said, stomping over to my chair.

Hannah grinned but Grace gave me a funny look.

'What?' I asked her.

'Was that about Jit?'

I nodded.

'Do you like *him* too?' she added.

'Yeah, but not like *that*. Jit's really cool. I used to think he was nuts but he can be really quite mature and clever and . . .'

I saw Grace pull a similar face to Imi.

'I told you – it's not like that!' I shouted.

'Easy now . . .' Hannah told me.

'I don't care, anyway,' said Grace, lying through her teeth. I knew she fancied Jit. Everyone did. And Jit fancied her too. The only people who couldn't work it out were Grace and Jit.

'Yes you do . . . but you've got it all wrong.'

Grace pretended to yawn.

'I'm bored now,' she told us. 'I'm going to go and find the lads.'

Then she walked out too. 'That's just great!' I told Hannah.

'I'm not saying anything,' she replied, although I could see that she wanted to.

# THREE

When I got home my dad was in the kitchen, making himself a sandwich with about three different cold meats.

'Isn't that pastrami?' I asked him as he loaded up a slice of thickly buttered bread.

'Yeah . . . I've never tried it before.'

'And chicken and ham?'

'So?'

'On buttered bread. With mayonnaise?'

My dad grinned at me. 'I'm hungry.'

'But you're not supposed to have butter. It's bad for you. And pastrami is made from beef, you know.'

My dad picked up a slice of the offending meat and stuffed it into his mouth.

'Tastes good though,' he told me, spitting bits of it everywhere.

'Dad!'

He ignored me, and smeared a big dollop of mayo

on the other slice before pushing it down to finish his sandwich.

'I thought Sikhs didn't eat beef?' I pointed out.

'Well . . . it's not like I'm a proper Sikh anyway. I'm sure one bit of beef won't send me to Hell. And what about those cheeseburgers you eat?'

'You bought me those.'

He grinned. 'Oh yeah.'

As he stood and ate his food, I wondered what he meant about not being a proper Sikh. Did that mean he wouldn't mind me seeing Imi? I wanted to ask him about it, but my mobile phone went off just as I was working up the courage. I looked at the screen to see Imi's name flashing next to a little bunch of flowers.

'That's the boyfriend?' mumbled my dad through another big mouthful of food.

'Suppose so,' I said, walking over to the kitchen door and out into the garden.

Our garden is quite big and I walked all the way down to the end of it, through some trees into a hidden bit at the back, talking to Imi. I arranged to meet him by some shops, which were round the corner from Grace's house. When I got back to the house my dad was just about to leave.

'I'm going back to the factory,' he told me, talking about one of the businesses that he ran with my mum. They also owned a cash and carry warehouse, three launderettes, about five houses that they rented out and a Punjabi clothing shop. I asked him where my mum was.

'Dunno . . . she's had to wait for a delivery at the cash and carry. Should be back in about half an hour.'

'I'm goin' out anyway,' I replied. 'But if you speak to her, tell her I'll be back about seven.'

'Yes, *madam*,' he told me.

Imi was standing outside the sports shop where my dad had bought me all of my gear over the years. I love sport and I'm kind of good at it. I pick things up really quickly too. At the moment I'm obsessed with badminton and football and I know that I'll be better than the lads soon. Even Dean, and he's almost as sporty as I am – although I always beat him at sprinting.

'Hi,' I said, as I walked up to my boyfriend.

'Hi.'

His voice was kind of flat but I didn't let it put me off. I was going to cheer him up whether he liked it or not. I gave him a kiss on the cheek.

'You OK now?' I asked, as he went a bit red. He nodded.

'I'm fine, now . . . sorry about before. I was acting like an idiot,' he admitted.

'Don't worry about it,' I said.

'So what do you want to do then?'

'Normal stuff . . . cinema maybe.'

He grinned. 'There's this great film on . . .'

'Well, let me call my mum and tell her I won't be in until even later,' I replied.

When I'd finished not answering my mum's questions about where I was going and all that stuff, I grabbed Imi's hand and we walked to a bus stop, one that was a long way from my parents' house.

Imi walked me halfway home before setting off for his own. We had a little set route that we took whenever we were in our own area, which involved us almost zigzagging our way through the streets before ending up near Grace's house. Then I went left and Imi went right. I didn't like having to sneak around but I hadn't plucked up the courage to tell my parents about Imi; and he hadn't told his parents about me either. When I got in, I thought about telling my mum there and then, only I bumped into my mental gran first.

'Where have you been? Don't you know that young girls shouldn't be out on their own? People will talk!' she spat at me in Punjabi.

'But I've been to my friend's house,' I replied.

'In my day . . .' she began, and went to find my mum. She was in the kitchen sitting with a cup of herbal tea, staring into space.

'What you doing – meditating?' I asked her.

'Not really,' she said, not looking up.

'Trouble at work?' I asked.

'Trouble, full stop,' she replied.

My heart sank for a second as I worried that she had found out about me and Imtiaz but it was something that was even more shocking.

'Mum?'

'I'm pregnant,' she replied, looking at me for the first time.

'What?'

'I'm pregnant . . . you know?'

'EURRGH!'

'Oh, don't be so silly,' she snapped.

'I just don't want to know . . . that's disgusting.'

My mum stood up and took my hands in hers.

'Aren't you excited? You're going to have a little brother or sister,' she said.

'Are *you* excited?' I asked in reply. 'You don't look it.'

She smiled and gave me a hug. 'Of course I am – it's just a bit of a shock.'

'You didn't plan it?'

She shrugged. 'Not really . . . we just kind of . . .'

'NO WAY! I don't want to know at all. I'm really happy and all of that stuff, but please . . . dirty old people!'

She pinched my cheeks, like she used to when I was a baby. Only it didn't hurt then because they were chubby. They weren't chubby any more though and it really did hurt but I kept a straight face.

'You'd better start thinking up some names,' she told me.

God – you think you *know* your parents and then they go and hit you with a brick.

# FOUR

'Paulo?' suggested Hannah the next day at school.

'What?' I asked, wondering what she was on about.

'*Names* . . . for your baby brother or sister? You did ask me for some.'

I shrugged. 'Oh yeah.'

'You freak. You only asked me like minus twenty million seconds ago!' she continued.

'Sorry, I was thinking about something else,' I told her.

'Your boyfriends?'

'Kind of. I want to tell my mum the truth about Imi but I don't know where to begin.'

'How about telling her that you mistakenly assumed she was prejudiced and so you've been telling her brazen, bare-faced lies ever since. Would that work?' she joked.

'Possibly not, Miss Meadows, but thanks for nothing!'

'Oh, why not just tell her you were scared?' Hannah suggested.

'Scared of what?'

'Anything,' she replied. 'When I was little and I did something naughty, I used to pretend to my mum I was scared. I used to just make up what I was scared of and every time she felt sorry for me and forgot to tell me off.'

'Don't think that'll do it either,' I sighed.

'Worked for me.'

We were sitting on a radiator in the main corridor, watching other pupils walk past. I hadn't seen Jit at all and was wondering where he was when two lads from our year, Robert and Wesley, came over and grinned at us like lunatics.

'Something to say, Mr Magoogan?' Hannah asked Wesley.

'You could say that,' replied Wesley, his smile widening even further. I didn't think people could open their mouths that wide.

'Are you going to tell us what it is?' continued Hannah. 'Or am I going to have to snog it out of Mr Sargeant?'

She was talking about Robert, who lost his smile for

a moment, went red, and stammered, 'Um . . . um . . . er . . .' he said, as Hannah winked at me.

'Spit it out, there's a good boy,' I said to him.

Wesley saved his friend from more embarrassment. 'We've been selected to play in a chess challenge for the school,' he told us.

Hannah groaned. 'Is that all? I thought you had something *really* interesting to tell us,' she moaned.

'It is!' said Robert, after he'd calmed down. 'It's a national challenge, held in Birmingham. Timed games against the best in the country. We're really very privileged.'

'And you're telling us because we've just spent the last year in isolation and find even the most mind-numbingly boring things interesting, I suppose?' I replied.

'Er . . .'

'Mr Black would like you to cover our selection and future progress in your little newspaper,' said Wesley.

'Oh, great!' said Hannah.

'That's what we thought,' replied Robert, thinking that he was agreeing with her but failing to notice the heavy edge of sarcasm in her voice. Typical boy.

'No,' explained Hannah, 'I didn't mean great as in *good* – I meant—'

'We'd love to,' I interrupted. 'Anything for the good of the school.'

'That's what we thought,' agreed Wesley.

'Still reading that fantasy series?' asked Hannah. '*The Dark Lord of Whatever . . .*?'

Robert and Wesley both beamed at the same time. 'It's wonderful!' said Wesley.

'But we're waiting for the sequels to be published,' added Robert.

'Although that *does* give us an opportunity to re-read the other books,' finished Wesley.

'Sequels?' I asked.

'There's gonna be two of them,' I heard Dean say from behind me.

'Hi, Dean!'

'Yeah . . . two more, and then two more, and eventually the whole of every bookshop and library is gonna be full of only those books.'

'Heaven,' sighed Robert.

'If that's as good as your idea of Heaven gets, you is in big trouble, you get me?' replied Dean, winking at me.

'But . . . I . . . er . . .' stammered Robert for the second time in five minutes.

'I mean, I'm thinking 'bout cars and gal and diamonds and ting, and there's you wit' a million books about the same messed-up fantasy world . . .' continued Dean.

'Well, *we* like them,' said Wesley.

And with that he grabbed Robert and they walked off.

'What about your article?' Hannah shouted after them but they didn't reply.

'Cheers, Dean,' I said. 'Now we're going to have to be nice to them.'

'Just flash a bit of leg,' he told me.

I punched him on the arm. 'OWW!'

'Oh, don't be such a girl!' laughed Hannah.

'If he was a girl he wouldn't have screamed. He's a little boy,' I told her.

'Kiss my—' he began, only he didn't finish.

Someone shouted, and then someone else screamed and Jit came running past us as fast as he could. Behind him an older lad, who looked like he was half skunk, was chasing; and behind him was Jason Patel.

'What the . . .?' shouted Dean, as he set off after Jit and the two older lads.

I looked at Hannah. 'I thought Jason Patel had been kicked out of school?' I asked.

'So did I.'

Two teachers went running past us too as I replied.

'So, what is he doing back at school?'

'Dunno,' said Hannah, jumping off the radiator, 'but I'm going to find out.'

I groaned and then followed her, as she followed the rest.

We didn't find them though. We walked all the way around the school but they had disappeared. And then it was time for our next lesson. Jit and Dean didn't show up for that either, but the Maths teacher, Mrs Lee-Cross, didn't even mention it. She was obviously aware of what was going on. Grace looked worried and, after the lesson, I asked her what had happened.

'Jit was talking to me when Jason Patel appeared out of nowhere and punched him,' she told me.

'Oh my God!' I replied, really concerned.

Grace gave me a funny look and then continued.

'He was with some other lad – the one with the

funny hair – and Jit ran off. They went after him.'

'But I thought that Jason had been kicked out.'

Grace shrugged. 'He's obviously come back for some reason.'

'Well, I'm gonna go and see Jit after school' I said. 'Make sure he's OK.'

'You don't need to do that,' Grace snapped. 'I'll do it. He was my friend first!'

'Grace, that's just being silly . . .'

'I don't care,' she replied. 'Since you started lying to your parents, I've hardly seen him. You don't have a special Jit-only licence.'

'But . . .' I began, realizing that she was really upset with me.

'Oh forget it,' she snapped again. 'I'm off to Art!'

I tried to speak to her all the way through our last lesson but she just ignored me and carried on painting. After school I went to the loo and when I got back to Hannah, Grace had gone.

'Her mum picked her up,' Hannah told me.

'I should call her – she's upset with me.'

Hannah shrugged. 'If I was you I'd leave it for a while. You know what she's like about Jit.'

'Yeah, but I'm not trying to take Jit away . . . we've just got quite close in the last few weeks, that's all.'

Once again my timing was rubbish. Just as I'd finished my last sentence, Imtiaz appeared next to me.

'Talking about your boyfriend again?' he asked.

'Oh don't be so silly – we were only—' I began.

'I couldn't care less,' he whined before he walked off too.

'This is getting silly now,' I told Hannah.

'Yep . . . sillier than a sun hat for cows.'

'Huh . . .?'

But she didn't explain. Instead she headed off out of school, past two Year Sevens who were pulling a rabbit along the corridor on a long leash.

'What *exactly* are you doing?' I asked them.

'Mind your own business,' squealed one of them.

'You lanky witch!' said the other.

'Charming,' I replied, storming off after Hannah.

# FIVE

The next day, I found out what was going on. I was in registration with Imi, who had calmed down, and Grace, who refused to tell me anything about what had happened to Jit and Dean.

'If you're so close to Jit, why hasn't he told you himself?' she sneered, like a little girl.

'You irritating little witch!' I replied.

'Oh, yeah – 'cos she's really gonna tell you if you call her names,' Hannah pointed out.

'I'm sorry, Grace,' I said.

Grace had been my friend since we'd met at infant school but she was a bit of a freak. Sometimes she'd be happy as anything and talking about silly stuff, and the next she'd get all arsey and behave like we were still infants. I knew she was upset so I let it go, hoping that I could make her see sense eventually. I didn't want to lose my oldest friend over a misunderstanding.

'Smelly bum,' she replied, making me want to strangle her all over again.

Eventually Mrs Dooher walked in with a really young-looking, skinny lad in tow. He had mad frizzy hair that stuck out at all different angles. I asked Imi who it was.

'I dunno – new kid?'

I looked back at the lad. His ears looked as though they were lop-sided and his glasses were too big for his face; and he had goofy teeth. I could see that the lads in class were going to have fun teasing him and I started to feel sorry for him before it had even happened. But my sympathy didn't last long.

'Suky?' said Mrs Dooher.

'Yes, miss?'

'This is Matthew . . . Matt Dribble . . . he's new,' she began.

'Not surprised he dribbles with teeth like that,' shouted Milorad.

'Be quiet!' warned Mrs Dooher.

'But, miss!' complained Milorad.

'Oh, go away!' Mrs Dooher half shouted, looking flustered.

'Do you want me to show him round?' I asked.

'Yes . . . you, and Jit – when he eventually arrives.'

I didn't want to, but I looked at Grace. It wasn't one of those looks that says 'Ha ha – I get to be with the boy you fancy,' but she took it that way, going red and turning her head. I tried to salvage the situation.

'But can't me and Imi do it?'

'You already are – doing it, innit?' shouted Dilip.

'Oh shut up, you immature little bed-wetter,' I told him.

'Oooooh!' said half the class.

'Bumpin' uglies!' shouted Raj, another lad.

'Calm down,' warned Mrs Dooher again, in her own quiet, rubbish sort of way.

'So, can we?' I repeated. 'Only Jit isn't here yet.'

'Yes I am!' said Jit, as he walked in with Dean in tow.

Mrs Dooher gave them a big smile, even though they were nearly late.

'What do you want me to do, miss?' he asked.

'Show our new boy, Matt, around. With Suky,' she told him.

Grace mumbled something under her breath but I ignored it.

'I don't mind,' said Jit. Then he saw Matt. His jaw fell open and he turned to Dean.

'Don't look at me, bro,' Dean told him. 'You is the one that offered.'

'You can both start your first lesson ten minutes late . . . I've cleared it. I want you to show him all around the school, but be quick. And then, can you let him hang around with you over break and lunch?'

'S'pose . . .' mumbled Jit, coming over to join the rest of us, as Hannah ran into the room.

'Sorry I'm late, miss,' she squirmed.

'Don't do it again,' said Mrs Dooher. See? Rubbish at discipline. Which is why we all loved her so much.

'What happened with Jason Patel?' asked Imi, as Dean and Jit sat down.

'It wasn't Jason,' Dean told us, as even Grace turned round to hear.

'Yes it was . . . we all saw him,' I replied.

Dean shook his head.

'It's even worse,' he said. 'That ugly bwoi you seen yesterday was *Justin* Patel – Jason's cousin.'

'What?'

'It's no lie,' said Jit. 'And he's brought an even uglier friend this time – Andy Stevenson.'

'The boy with hair that looked like a skunk's arse?' asked Hannah.

'Yeah – him!' growled Jit.

'But why are they after you two?' said Imi.

'Revenge,' explained Dean. 'We're in the dog do, big time, you get me?'

'That's just silly,' I told him. 'Mr Black won't put up with people from outside coming in and causing trouble.'

'That's just it,' added Jit, as Grace pulled another face. 'They're new pupils . . . them man are part of the school.'

Right on cue, Matt walked over to us and sat in the only available chair.

'Hello!' said Hannah, smiling at him.

'Hi . . .' said Matt, in a high-pitched voice.

'Where are you from then?'

Matt shrugged and said nothing.

'*Well?*' asked Dean. ''Cos if you wanna sit with the cool people you need to get with the programme, you get me?'

'Oh,' said Matt. 'I think I get you . . .'

When he opened his mouth to speak, I saw that two of his teeth were dark yellow and that he had bits of food stuck between them. I cringed.

'So, let's start again,' said Dean. 'How you doin',
Matty, my man?'

'I'm fine,' he replied.

'And which part of this fair city have you come
from?'

'Round Belgrave way,' he told us.

'An' what—?' began Dean, only for Mrs Dooher to
tell him to shut up.

'But I'm just bein' nice, miss . . .' he complained.

I saw Dilip and Mohammed smirk and waited for
them to tease someone. 'Suky's always nice, miss.
Maybe Dribble-pants can be her third boyfriend?'

They giggled and Matt went red.

'I'm gonna stick that pen you're holding up your
nose in a minute,' warned Jit.

'Try it!' challenged Dilip, in his whiny voice. 'I'll tell
miss—'

Jit pushed back his chair and Dilip flinched.

'See how you jump,' laughed Dean. 'Weasel . . .'

'*Miss!*' squealed Dilip.

Miss Dooher sighed, told us to shut up again and
took the register.

Jit showed Matt where the boys' toilets were after

registration because he was dying to use the loo.

'I've got a bladder problem,' he told us.

Jit grinned at me as we waited for him in the corridor. 'That bwoi is unfortunate,' he told me.

'Jit – that's not fair . . . he's new,' I said.

'And funny looking!'

'Don't be mean,' I said, before asking him some more about Justin Patel and Andy Stevenson.

'They told me that they were going to make my life a misery,' grinned Jit. 'Like I ain't had that already.'

He was talking about the trouble he'd had with his mum's last boyfriend, Micky, who had been a bully. But Jit had come up with a plan to get rid of him and it had worked.

'You need to be careful though,' I told him. 'They might hurt you.'

I put my hand on his arm and then, realizing that I'd done it, I pulled away. Jit gave me a funny look and then looked away.

'They ain't nuttin',' he told me. 'I can handle them.'

'Ooh macho boy,' I grinned.

'You mean, man?' he corrected.

'Uh-uh – I mean boy,' I replied.

'Cheeky cow!'

'Oi!'

I pushed him playfully into the wall, which is when my bad timing came back and hit me on the head. Jit grabbed my arm as I pushed him and I kind of fell into him, just as the door to the girls' toilets opened and Puspha, a girl in our form, walked out. She looked at us, grinned and then started to giggle.

'Wait till I tell everyone else!' she said.

'But it's not what you think!' I protested.

'Yeah, yeah,' she said, walking back to her lesson.

'But . . .'

Jit let go of my arm.

'Don't worry about it,' he told me. 'We were just messing about.'

I shrugged.

'That's not how she's gonna tell it,' I said.

Jit shrugged too.

'Who cares?' he said.

In my head I went through a list of names. Grace, Imi, my parents; but I didn't say anything out loud.

'What the hell is he doing in there?' asked Jit.

'Er . . . it's a loo. What do people usually do in the loo?' I replied. 'No, second thoughts – scratch that. I don't wanna think about it.'

'I'm going to make sure he ain't fallen down the plug hole,' said Jit. 'Seeing as how he's that skinny.'

I watched him walk in and after a few seconds heard a loud braying, like a donkey on laughing gas. Then Jit walked out into the corridor.

'Man – you hear that laugh?' he asked me.

'Yeah – is that Matt?'

Jit nodded. 'I told him to hurry up or we might bump into Santa Claus and he did *that*!'

'What – laughed?'

'If that's what you'd call it,' he said.

The toilet door opened and Matt walked out.

'That *wewey* was a *vewy* funny joke,' he said, as I realized that he had a speech thing. He couldn't pronounce 'r' properly. I hadn't noticed it in class earlier on, but it was very pronounced. Or *pwonounced* even . . .

'Yes it was,' grinned Jit, sensing the chance to make fun of Matt. '*Wewey, wewey* funny. Mr Dwibbler has got a sense of humour . . .'

I shook my head and punched Jit on the arm again. The idiot.

# SIX

The following Saturday morning I had to get up early and go shopping with my dad. We went to our local Asda, and I spent most of the time there avoiding bumping into people. It was packed and everyone in there was annoying me, including my dad, who was going around picking up things that weren't on the shopping list.

'Never tried this,' he said for about the fiftieth time, holding up a small jar of pesto.

'Yes you have. We have it on pasta all the time,' I pointed out.

'Not this one, we don't. This is handmade in Italy and it's got sun-ripened tomatoes in it.'

'That's what it says on the label,' I replied. 'But I bet it's just the normal stuff only more expensive.'

'And this too,' he said, putting the pesto back and picking up a bottle of chilli oil.

'But it's just olive oil with chillies in it,' I told him.

'Sound's good to me.'

I sighed. 'Mum made some last year and you never touched it.'

He looked at me and shook his head. 'Nah – if there had been this kind of oil at home, I would have used it,' he told me.

'Oh shut up, you stupid old man!'

I pushed our trolley on up the aisle, narrowly avoiding an old dear who tried to ram into my side.

'Oh, watch out!' I shouted.

The old dear stuck two fingers up at me and went on her way, mumbling something in Hindi. I steered into the next aisle, where the cans of baked beans and tuna were, and walked straight into Imtiaz's mum.

'Hello, Suky!' she beamed at me. Behind her, I saw Imi with his dad, looking at something on the shelf.

'Hi!' I said, as my stomach dropped down to my feet and it suddenly got harder to breathe.

'Are you OK – you look ill?' Imi's mum asked.

I gulped down some air and tried to stay calm. My dad was only on the next aisle. 'I'm fine – just bored with the shopping,' I half lied.

Mrs Dhondy smiled and then looked over my shoulder.

'Ah! Mrs Dhondy,' said my dad, so loud that every-one in the entire place stopped to stare. Well, OK – may-be not *everyone*. Imi and his dad heard him though.

'And how are you?' continued my dad, as Imi and his father walked up to us.

'Fine, Mr Singh,' replied Imi's mum. 'And you?'

'Can't complain,' said my dad, shaking Imi's dad's hand and having the same conversation over again.

I tried to smile at Imi but it came out all wonky and wrong.

'Hey,' he said, looking out of the corner of his eye at my dad and then back at me.

'And Imtiaz . . . looking fit and strong!' boomed my dad. Foghorn in shorts – that's what he is.

'Hi, Mr Singh,' Imi replied, looking all shy.

'We never see you any more,' continued my dad. 'You used to come over all the time . . . grown up now though, eh? Got other things on your mind!'

'Er . . . yeah,' said Imi.

Mr Dhondy asked after my mum and then told me how tall I was getting.

'You'll be just like your dad, won't she, Randeep?'

My dad grinned.

'Not as ugly, though,' I said, smiling.

'Cheeky bleeder!' replied my dad.

I glanced at Imi again but he gave me a funny look, like he was embarrassed or something, and then he looked away.

'Suky's got herself a boyfriend,' my dad told them, the idiot.

'Oh yes? That's lovely,' said Imi's mum. 'What's his name?'

'Jit,' said my dad.

Imi's parents looked at each other and then at their son. I thought they were going to say something negative but they didn't. Instead Imi's mum said that Imi had a girlfriend too.

'Only natural at his age,' said my dad, still competing for the World's Loudest Voice trophy.

'Yes – that's my view entirely,' said Mr Dhondy. 'She's very similar to Suky from what my son tells me . . .'

I shot Imi a dirty look, but he didn't look at me.

'Oh – then he has good taste too,' said my dad.

'You know – I always thought that these two might get together,' said Imi's mum. 'Tina and I used to joke about it.'

My dad shrugged. 'Probably too much like brother and sister,' he pointed out.

'Perhaps,' replied Mrs Dhondy, smiling at me.

After a few more words, Imi and his family moved on and I told him that I'd call him later.

'About that school project,' I lied.

'What school project?' he asked, the stupid boy.

'About the newspaper?'

Imi registered about five seconds later.

'Oh yeah, that,' he said, sounding completely guilty. He was no good at this secretive lark.

'I've got a lot of questions for you,' I said sharply. 'And I'd love to know all about this new girlfriend of yours.'

'You mean he hasn't told you?' asked his mum.

'No – he must have forgotten,' I said.

'I think he's made her up,' joked Mr Dhondy.

That was when my heart tried to force its way out of my nostrils. I was so relieved when me and dad walked away to finish our shopping.

Later on, I told my mum that we'd bumped into the Dhondys.

'Oh – how nice. How was Mariam? I haven't spoken to her for ages.'

'She's fine,' I said.

'Did you tell her our good news?'

'Oh it's good news now then?' I asked.

'Always was, although we haven't told your gran yet,' she told me.

'And . . .?'

'And we don't want her to find out just yet, so keep that big mouth of yours shut,' she warned.

'But she's nuts – she won't know what I'm on about,' I argued.

My mum shifted in her chair and changed the subject. 'I should really call Mariam – tell her about the baby,' she said.

'I could tell Imi if you like?'

'You mean you haven't already?' she asked, looking surprised.

I shook my head. 'Only the girls . . . it's far too embarrassing,' I said.

'Oh, Suky, don't be such a nerd!'

'MUM!'

She smiled and told me to make her a cup of tea. I

went into the kitchen where my gran was peeling an onion.

'What's that for?' I asked her in Punjabi, the only language she could speak.

'What's it to you?' she snapped, not looking at me.

'Gran!'

She turned to me and pointed the little knife she was using threateningly.

'I know,' she told me. 'Don't think I don't know . . . you're all after my money. Trying to kill me with poisoned food!'

'You're totally bonkers,' I told her, this time in English.

'See?' she shouted. 'You talk to me in that peasant language . . . I *know*!'

And with that, she left the kitchen, taking her onion and the knife with her. I stood where I was for a moment and imagined her stabbing us all to death and then drinking our blood. But that was the kind of thing Grace would imagine, so I shook my head, stopped being so silly and made the tea, wondering all the while whether insanity ran in our family.

\* \* \*

Imi rang me later that evening, asking me if I wanted to go out for a while.

'OK – where shall we meet?' I asked.

'Down by the shops, round the corner from Grace's?' he suggested.

'Cool. I'll be ten minutes.'

We met outside a bookshop called Browsers and walked past the rest of the shops, down an alleyway and onto Holmfield Avenue, which led down onto Holmfield Road. There was a little brook that ran under the road and we stood by it and had a snog. Then we sat on a wall and talked about stuff. I told him about the trip to the seaside that my dad had planned and that I'd asked Jit to come along.

'This pretence is gonna have to stop soon,' he told me.

'I know,' I replied, looking down at the brook.

'You're going to have to tell them.'

'Well what about you and your "girlfriend" – what's that all about?' I asked.

'They don't know it's you,' he admitted. 'But they want to meet my girlfriend and I'm having to tell almost as many lies as you.'

'I'm not lying exactly,' I protested.

Imi shrugged. 'Yeah – you're just jugglin',' he said quietly.

'I'm sorry,' I told him, before taking his hand in mine.

'You and Jit just seem to be getting closer and closer. I feel like I'm being left behind,' he said.

'But you're my boyfriend,' I replied. 'I don't want to go out with Jit. He's a really nice lad – different when you get to know him, but I don't like him in that way!'

I leaned across and kissed him a few times, not noticing the two bikes pull up across the road. When I did look over, I saw Justin Patel and his even uglier friend, Andy.

They were sneering at us, and for a moment I thought they were going to come over and bother us, but they didn't. They just rode off, laughing.

'They're horrible,' I told Imi, when they had gone.

'I know. And what's up with Andy's hair?'

'I dunno,' I admitted.

'So has Jit said yes to the family day out?' he asked, changing the subject.

'Not yet,' I said. 'I'm going to chase it up at school on Monday.'

Imi smiled and gave me another kiss before replying.

'As long as you ain't chasing *him*,' he told me, smiling again.

'Never.'

I should have given more thought to Justin and his mate but at the time I didn't realize just how nasty they really were. That would change quite soon though.

# SEVEN

The following Monday I was sitting in English with Grace and Hannah, waiting for our first lesson to start, when Jit walked in sporting a black eye. For a minute I thought that things had gone bad at home again, but when I asked him he shrugged and said, 'Justin.'

'When did he do that?' asked Grace, looking really concerned.

'Yesterday,' Jit told her. 'I was walking down Evington Road, going to Dean's, and he jumped me.'

'Have you told anyone?' I asked. It was a stupid question though.

'I ain't grassing up no one,' he told me. 'It's finished with anyway.'

'You can't let him bully you like that,' insisted Grace. 'It's not fair!'

Jit shrugged. 'Fair ain't got nothing to do with it,' he said.

As he spoke, Mr Herbert walked in wearing a long

black leather coat. He looked like someone in an old war film – like a Gestapo officer or something.

'Suits his personality,' whispered Hannah.

'You're telling me,' I whispered back.

'SHUT UP!' shouted Mr Herbert.

'Are they the only words you know?' I muttered.

'I beg your pardon?' asked Herbert.

I thought really quickly about something that rhymed with what I'd just said, just like Dean would do, but nothing came to mind. Instead I just sat where I was like an idiot. Herbert walked over to our table and sneered at me with his bug eyes.

'I think detention at lunch time for you, Miss Kaur.'

I looked away from him and at Jit, who was smiling.

'You're a dick, you know that?' he said to Herbert, under his breath.

'I'm sorry – something to say, Jit?' asked the teacher.

'Yeah,' said Jit, louder this time. 'I said . . . why can't you just be nice to people?'

Mr Herbert's face began to turn a deep red that spread slowly from his neck upwards. By the time it got to his forehead, he was fuming.

'Detention for you too!' he squealed, trying to control himself.

Jit shrugged. 'Whatever . . .'

I turned to look at Grace, who was glaring at me. I smiled but she didn't even flinch. Knowing her, she probably thought we'd done it on purpose, just to be together at lunch time.

'Right – enough of the cabaret . . . get your books out. NOW!' said Mr Herbert.

I was in Mr Herbert's classroom, starting detention, when our English teacher walked in and smiled at me, like a weasel.

'You really shouldn't let people like Jit deflect you from your studies,' he told me.

'I don't,' I replied, looking out of the window.

'You're one of the most intelligent people in the class,' he continued. 'Don't get dragged down by a waster like Jit.'

I spun round and looked at him in disgust. How could he call someone he was supposed to be teaching a waster? If he already had that view of Jit – then how could he teach him properly? I wanted to ask him but knew that it would only get me into more trouble. So

I said nothing and returned to looking out of the window. Jit walked in a few seconds afterwards and I smiled at him.

'All right, Suky?' he said, sitting down on the chair next to mine.

'Yeah,' I replied with a smile.

Mr Herbert told us to keep quiet and said that he was going to leave us there for a while.

'The door is open and Mr Singh is in the next room, so if you start messing about . . .' he warned.

'Yeah, yeah,' murmured Jit.

'And there'll be two more pupils joining you in about five minutes. Now sit quietly and think about why you're here today . . . how you can improve your behaviour until it fits the notion of "civilized".'

'Whatever you say, you get me?' said Jit.

Mr Herbert shook his head and walked out of the room.

'Why can't you just keep quiet when he's around?' I asked Jit.

'Because he's an idiot,' he replied.

'Yeah – he is. But all you do is get into trouble all the time. Don't you want to do well at school?'

'Yeah – I do, but not if I have to pretend that

people like him are OK. He hates me anyway.'

I was about to say that he didn't, but stopped when I remembered what Herbert had said about Jit. Instead I changed the subject.

'My dad wants to know if you can come on our family day out,' I told him.

Jit shrugged. 'I dunno, Suky. Grace is being funny with me and Imi keeps giving me dirty looks. I reckon we should come clean.'

'But just this one last time,' I pleaded. 'I'm going to tell them soon anyway. Me and dad saw Imi and his family shopping at the weekend and they get on really well. I think my old man would be OK—'

'So, tell him that I'm just your blag boyfriend then.'

I sighed. 'I *will* . . . after the trip maybe.'

'But . . .'

'*Please*, Jit!'

He looked at me and then winked.

'OK . . . but this is the last time for definite,' he told me.

'Promise,' I said. 'It'll be so cool to finally stop pretending that *you're* my boyfriend and tell them about Imtiaz.'

Jit raised an eyebrow. 'Why? What's wrong with me?' he asked, pretending to be sad.

'Oh, don't be such a saddo!' I told him.

He got up and, before I could stop him, grabbed me in a shoulder lock, tickling me.

'Who you callin' saddo?' he asked, as I struggled to get away.

I managed to get my arms around his middle and drag him towards me, but he had a good hold on me. I don't like being outdone by boys, so I started struggling even more and in the end I fell backwards off the chair and onto the floor, with Jit on top of me. He soon let me go after that, going red in the face and scrambling off me.

'Sorry,' he muttered.

'It's OK,' I told him. 'Not like you're strong or anything.'

'You can say that again,' came a sneering voice from the door.

We looked up and saw Justin and Andy standing in the doorway, smiling like vultures that had spotted a carcass.

'We could see you was busy,' said Andy. 'We didn't want to disturb you.'

He smiled his nasty smile at me again and I wanted to be sick. Then I caught sight of his hair, which was black with a big white patch right in the middle.

'Who does your hair?' I heard myself saying. 'A senile gorilla with a bottle of bleach?'

Andy stepped towards us and Jit stood up quickly.

'Don't get your knickers in a twist,' said Justin, behind him. 'We're not here for you. We've got detention with Herbert.'

Jit didn't say anything, but Justin and Andy sat down and continued to look at us.

Justin sneered. 'That eye looks bad, Jit. Someone hit you?'

Jit pulled a chair out next to me and sat down, ignoring Justin, as Mr Herbert walked back into the room. I'd never been so pleased to see him. Justin spent the rest of the detention watching me. Even when I wasn't looking in his direction, which was most of the time, I could feel his eyes on me. It wasn't a good feeling.

The bad feeling I'd had got worse between my final two lessons. I was walking out of the loos when I saw Justin and Andy standing by a radiator. I tried to walk past but Andy stood in my way. He was almost as ugly as Justin. He had one of those whispy moustaches that some boys get and a big mole next to his nose, with a long hair growing out of it. There was a musty, sweaty smell coming from him.

'Get out of my way,' I told him.

He grinned at me, showing off disgusting yellow teeth.

He really was minging.

'I said move—'

Justin stepped towards me, as Andy stayed where he was. I looked around but there was no one else in the corridor and I started to get scared. Justin smiled before he spoke.

'You're a right slapper,' he told me. 'I mean *two* boyfriends – what's that all about?'

'Yeah . . . proper slapper, you get me?' added Andy. His breath smelled bad, like maybe he had a dead animal in his mouth, and I wanted to throw up.

'You don't know anything about me,' I told them defiantly.

'Yes we do. One day we see you with that Imtiaz, snogging him up in broad daylight; and the next, you're all over Jit,' said Justin.

'But—' I began.

'So, we asked around and a couple of lads in your class told us what we wanted to know, Suky. Although they had to be persuaded,' he cut in.

'Now, what would happen if your parents found out about Jit?' said Andy.

'Serious trouble, I reckon,' added Justin.

I couldn't help glaring at him, even though I didn't want him to see that I was worried.

'And seein' as how we followed you home the other day when you were feeling up Imtiaz, it's not like we don't know where to post an anonymous letter,' he threatened.

'Get lost!' I replied.

'Won't cost you much . . . twenty quid a week should do it,' said Andy. 'Your parents must be rich – yer house is big enough.'

'You think I'm going to pay you?' I said. 'You're mad.'

Justin stepped right into my face.

'Either you pay or we tell your parents about how much you lie, and we'll tell Imtiaz what you were doing with Jit during detention.'

I glared at him. 'You stupid—' I started.

'You got until Friday to get us the money,' said Andy, cutting me off. They smiled again and walked off, leaving me in shock.

There was no way I was going to give them my money but I couldn't risk them telling my parents or Imtiaz anything. I was in trouble.

# EIGHT

The next morning, before registration, I told Grace and Hannah most of what had happened, but not everything. I didn't mention that Justin and Andy had seen me rolling around the floor with Jit. Grace would have *loved* that. Instead I told them that they had threatened to lie to Imi about me and Jit.

'What kind of lies?' asked Grace.

'They're gonna tell Imi that they saw me and Jit snogging but that never happened,' I told her.

'So, they're just making it all up, are they?' she replied.

'Yes!'

'Just so that you'll give them money?' added Hannah.

'Exactly. And they actually followed me home too, so they know where I live.'

'That's just creepy,' said Hannah. 'Can't you tell a teacher?'

'And say what? It's their word against mine – no one else was in the corridor.'

'And you really *haven't* been seeing Jit too?' asked Grace.

'Grace . . . I just told you the truth!'

She looked at me, raised an eyebrow and then shrugged. 'OK – I believe you,' she said. 'We're going to have to tell the lads though.'

'Why?' I asked.

'Because that way they won't believe any lies that those two ugly munters come up with,' Hannah pointed out.

'Forewarned is forearmed and all that,' added Grace.

'But what if they tell my parents?'

'That's another problem entirely,' replied Grace.

'So, what are we going to do about it,' I asked.

Both of my friends shrugged.

'Dean and Jit are always good for coming up with ideas. Let's have a conference round at Grace's later,' suggested Hannah.

'Yeah!' agreed Grace. 'Surely we can come up with something between us? I mean – those two are thicker than pig poo!'

'Whale poo, even,' added Hannah.

'Elephant and whale poo *together* isn't as thick as them,' said Grace.

Mrs Dooher walked in and said hello, as I sat and thought about what we were going to do. I suppose it was my fault for lying to my parents but that still didn't excuse what Justin and Andy were doing. I wanted to go and kick them in their heads, I was so angry.

'How did it go with Matt?' asked Mrs Dooher, disrupting my thoughts.

'Huh?'

'Matt . . . the *new* boy?' she said.

I'd totally forgotten about him.

'Er . . . he was OK,' I told her. 'We showed him around and then he did his own thing, kind of.'

Mrs Dooher shook her head.

'You mean you ignored him from then on.'

'Not exactly,' I said, trying to remember the last time I had seen him, which was when he'd been talking to Robert and Wesley about those silly books that they all loved.

'I think he's hanging around with Robert and Wesley from 8CM, miss.'

'Yeah, he is,' added Grace. 'I saw him this morning. They were talking about science . . . he's going to fit right in with them.'

'Oh, good,' replied Mrs Dooher, genuinely.

'Do I get an award for integrating him so success-fully into our school?' I asked her.

'You should get an award for the skinniest legs!' shouted a lad called Paresh. I turned round and gave him a filthy look.

'Oooh – I'm scared,' he said in a girly voice.

I waited until Mrs Dooher was distracted before I made my move. I got up and walked over to Paresh. He smiled at me. I shot out my arm, grabbed his big, long nose and twisted it.

'OWWWWWWW!!!'

The rest of his mates started laughing, and Mrs Dooher looked up from what she was doing.

'Are you beating up the boys again?' she asked.

'Yes, miss,' I replied, grinning because I knew what was coming.

'Oh good,' said Mrs Dooher. 'Saves me a job . . .'

I didn't even make it to lunch time before Justin and

Andy lived up to their threats. I was walking into my CDT class when I saw Imi. He was holding Jit by his throat and pushing him up against a wall. Dean was trying to pull them apart. I ran over and grabbed Imi's arm, shouting at him to let go.

'What's going on – stop it!' I shouted.

'I *know* you've been seeing my girl!' spat Imi, right in Jit's face.

Jit shoved Imi back, and between me and Dean we managed to make him let go, only Imi didn't calm down. Instead he turned on me.

'You were *seen* – kissing Jit,' he told me angrily.

'No I *wasn't* – it's a lie!' I told him.

'Why would they lie?' he asked. 'They saw you!'

'*Who?*' asked Dean, holding Jit back with one hand.

Jit was going mad, swearing and trying to get at Imi.

'Cool it!' Dean shouted at him.

'This is all wrong,' I said, trying not to cry.

'Well, what happened then?' demanded Imi.

'It was Justin and Andy – they've been threatening me. They said that if I didn't give them money they'd tell you a load of lies.'

Imi thought about it for a moment – just enough time for Jit to jump on him.

'OI!' shouted Dean, pulling Jit off.

'You think I'm scared of you?' Jit asked Imi.

I grabbed Jit by the hand and told him to stop. 'It's not his fault . . . it was Justin!' I repeated.

'So?' replied Jit. 'He could have asked me first. Instead he jumped me like he's some bad bwoi . . . ain't no one grabbing me up like that!'

The rest of the pupils were beginning to come into the classroom and they looked shocked. Apart from Marco, that is. He told Jit to smack Imi.

'I'm going to stick your head in a vice in a minute,' Dean warned.

Marco went red and looked at the floor.

'Just calm down,' Dean told Imi and Jit. 'Otherwise I'm gonna bang *both* of you out!'

'It isn't what you think,' I told Imi, who was beginning to calm down.

'Then what is it?' he asked me.

'A lie – that's all . . . I was telling Grace and Hannah about it and we were going to tell you all.'

'What the *hell* is going on?' shouted Mr Granger from the doorway.

'Nothing, sir,' I lied.

'Doesn't look like nothing to me,' he replied. 'Imtiaz – why is your tie all over the place?'

Imi looked at me and over at Jit. He turned to Mr Granger and shrugged.

'We were just messing about,' he told him.

'Yeah – practising rugby tackles,' added Dean. 'Like we seen the England team doing.'

'Jit?' asked Granger.

'Yeah – *that* was it,' snapped Jit, still angry.

I looked at him. 'Just leave it, Jit,' I whispered. 'It was a misunderstanding.'

He nodded at me but his eyes were glazed over and I knew he wasn't listening. As Grace and Hannah walked in, I sat down with Imi and tried to talk to him. But Mr Granger had started the lesson and Imi was ignoring me. Instead, I wrote a note for Grace, telling her what had happened, and passed it along. She sent one back and then over the rest of the lesson we had a conversation that way. Grace told me that she'd talk to Dean and Jit, and ask them to come to her house after school. I agreed to do the same with Imi. We really had to sort out the mess that I'd created. I didn't want Imi and Jit to fight. We were all friends and I wanted it to stay that way.

# NINE

We arranged with Grace that Dean and Jit would arrive at her house before the rest of us. I went home first and walked straight into another problem. My dad was in the living room, eating a banana and watching kids' telly.

'How 'bout this comin' Saturday?' he asked me, as I flopped down onto the sofa.

'It's the day after Friday,' I replied. 'You can't miss it . . . just wake up and there it'll be!'

'For the family day trip,' he added.

'Oh right – that.'

'Well? I've spoken to your mum and she's up for it. And your uncle Mandeep is coming too, bringing the family.'

'Whatever,' I replied, yawning at him.

'So, is the lad coming or not?' he said, talking about Jit.

'Er . . . yeah, I think so.' I was thinking about my

**229**

troubles and my dad may as well have been talking into a hurricane.

'Have you actually asked him, Suky?'

'Yeah . . .'

My dad sighed and stood up. He placed his banana skin on the coffee table.

'You been takin' drugs or summat?' he asked me.

'Don't be silly,' I replied.

'So, is he coming?'

I nodded. 'I'm going to see him later so I'll double check, but he did say he was going to come.'

'Oh good,' said my dad, with a sly smile. 'We can have lots of fun!'

I gave him a funny look.

'Don't be mean to him – otherwise I'll tell him not to bother,' I warned.

'Mean – me? Never. It's your gran he needs to be careful with.'

'*Your* mother,' I reminded him.

As if she had sensed that we'd mentioned her, my gran came walking into the room, muttering under her breath.

'What's that, Mum?' asked my dad in Punjabi.

'Nothing you need to hear,' she told him. 'Isn't this

witch supposed to be at school?' she added, talking about me.

'She's been and come back,' he told her.

'Finished already?' replied my gran. 'What kind of school is it? They should beat them with sticks . . . straighten them right out.'

'Not in this country,' I told her, speaking in English because I knew she'd react.

'Shall I paint your face white?' she asked me in Punjabi. 'Talking to me in that silly language all the time.'

Then she looked at my dad, farted twice and walked out of the room, talking to my granddad, who'd been dead since I was four years old.

'You going to put that in the bin?' I asked my dad.

'What . . . your gran?' he replied, with a grin.

'No, you fool. The banana skin!' I replied, laughing.

'Nah – give you something to do instead of sitting on your arse all day watching telly,' he said.

'Look who's talking.'

'I'm off to work now,' he replied. 'Someone's gotta pay for your expensive tastes.'

'Oh go and eat another banana,' I told him.

He walked out of the room, doing a bad impression of an ape. The weirdo.

Grace's dad opened the door to me, Imi and Hannah about an hour later. He was wearing an apron and yellow rubber gloves.

'Hi, Mr Parkhurst,' said Hannah.

'Hello – please excuse the outfit. I was cleaning the bath.'

'No problem,' I told him.

'They're downstairs playing pool,' he told us before wandering off.

Grace's parents had turned their cellar into a proper room when we were all kids, and it was massive. It ran almost the entire length of their house and the ceiling was quite high. There were sofas down there, along with a telly and hi-fi; and a pool table that the lads always hogged whenever we visited, which was all the time. Especially Jit, who seemed to spend more time at Grace's house than his own.

As we made our way downstairs, I hoped that Jit wouldn't throw a fit when he saw Imi. Grace hadn't told him we were coming and I didn't want it to be an unpleasant surprise. It wasn't. Jit nodded at Imi when he saw him and Imi said hello. It was all cold and macho, but then what did I expect from boys? It's not like they were going to hug each other or something.

'You made it then?' said Grace, as I joined her on a sofa.

'Yeah,' I replied.

Dean was bent across the table, about to take a shot when Hannah tried to put him off.

'Like two pigs fighting in a sack,' she said to us.

'What is?' I asked.

'Dean's ass . . . it's huge!' she replied.

Dean missed his shot by a mile and turned to her.

'See? You just put me off, Hannah.'

'Well your *ass* was putting *me* off,' she told him.

Dean grinned. 'No it wasn't. You love it . . . I seen the way you look at it . . . well you can look, darlin', because yuh nah get none ah me!'

Hannah pretended that she was puking.

'You can keep it,' she said, when she'd stopped pretending.

'Yeah,' added Grace. 'He can keep it from falling *out* with a harness and a big tarpaulin.'

'*Huge* tarpaulin,' said Hannah.

'Giant . . . big enough to hold a *tank*!'

Dean just grinned again. 'If I had known it was pick-on-Dean day – I would have stayed at home,' he said.

I smiled and looked over at Jit and Imi. They were standing at opposite ends of the table, not talking and not looking at each other either. I caught Jit's eye and nodded my head towards Imi, hoping that he'd make the first move. Some chance. Jit just shrugged and looked away. In the end, as Dean, Grace and Hannah continued to tease each other, I decided to get things going.

'We need to talk,' I said, in my loudest voice.

'Someone let a ferry in here?' asked Dean. 'I heard a foghorn.'

'Listen, you chicken-legged wannabe-but-can't-rhyme rapper – this is serious,' I replied.

'*Oooh* – let's all sit down because Suky says so,' added Hannah.

'Oh come on – it's not funny,' I told them seriously.

Everyone looked at me and shut up. Hannah and Dean went and sat on the other sofa, and Jit and Imi stayed where they were.

'So what's goin' on?' asked Dean.

'What do you mean – what's going on?' asked Grace. 'Just the little matter of two of us trying to beat each other to a pulp at school – that's all.'

'Weren't *my* fault,' said Jit.

'Weren't mine either,' added Imi.

I sighed. 'It wasn't either of you. It was all down to Justin Patel and his smelly mate!'

'He *does* smell, doesn't he?' said Grace. 'And what's the deal with that hair?'

Dean smirked. 'I know how that happened,' he told us. 'This girl I know, in Year Ten – she told me.'

'What – one of your pretend women?' asked Hannah.

'No pretence at all, my dear,' replied Dean, in a posh accent.

'So how did it happen?' asked Jit.

Dean sat up and cleared his throat, like he was about to tell us something really important.

'That Andy was watchin' some telly show and decided that he wanted to have bleached hair, just like one of the characters. Thought it'd help him pull girls and that. He told Justin, and Justin said that he'd do it for him. Told him it was easy and he'd done it before. So Andy takes his skinny, no-ass body round to Justin's and they start trying to bleach his hair—'

'They tried to use a home bleaching kit?' I asked.

Dean shook his head. 'Nah – that would have been too normal,' he told us.

'So, what *did* they use?' asked Imi, smiling at me.

'Domestos,' replied Dean, with a grin.

'NO!' shouted Hannah.

'*Yeah* – Justin poured a load of Domestos over Andy's head, and when it started to burn his scalp he ran out of the house screaming. They had to take him to hospital!'

'But couldn't he just shave his head and let it grow back as his natural colour?' asked Grace.

Dean shook his head.

'Nah – the girl I know told me that he's damaged summat permanently and it won't go back to normal.'

'That's just stupid,' said Hannah.

'Very stupid,' I added. 'But none of this helps us sort out the mess we're in.'

'You mean the mess *you're* in?' asked Grace.

'Whatever,' I replied. 'Can we try and sort it out please?'

Dean slumped back again.

'OK,' he said, 'although I was about to tell you another story I know.'

'About Justin and Andy?' asked Grace excitedly.

'Nah – 'bout this next idiot—'

'*Dean!*' I snapped.

'OK, OK. No need to get your size eighteen panties in a twist!' he replied.

# TEN

'So what we going to do then?' I asked.

'Dunno,' replied Grace.

'What did they say to you exactly?' asked Dean.

'They said that they'd tell Imtiaz that I was seeing Jit too,' I began.

'Well, they already done that,' said Jit. 'And macho-man over there reacted too.'

Imi tensed up but then calmed straight down.

'I know he was wrong to have a go at you,' said Grace, 'but he didn't know they were lying.'

Jit had probably been expecting Grace to back him up. I think it made him pay attention a bit more.

'And if someone had told me that my boyfriend was seen snogging some other girl, I would have reacted the same way,' she added.

'Can't see you grabbing someone by the throat and

holding them against a wall,' Dean pointed out.

'Oh, you know what I mean,' replied Grace, seriously.

'So, we need to square that first,' said Hannah. She looked at Jit and Imi in turn.

'Don't look at me,' said Imi. 'He jumped me after I'd stopped and anyway – I'm not the one going on and on about it.'

'Oh don't be such a child,' I told him. 'Both of you are to blame for the way you reacted but neither of you started it. That was Justin and Andy.'

'But I never done anything wrong,' Jit pointed out. 'Why should I get grief? He grabbed my throat for no reason!'

'We *have* been spending a lot of time together,' I told him. 'And we were messing about when they saw us.'

It was a gamble, being honest about what Justin and Andy had seen, but I decided that I didn't have anything to hide. After all, as I'd said, me and Jit had been messing about. Jit went a bit red as Imi gave me a quizzing look.

'What do you mean *messing* about?' he asked.

'Jit was tickling me,' I admitted. 'It was just a bit of fun, that's all.'

'*Tickling* you? And you think that's OK?' he snapped.

'Oh – don't be such a baby,' said Grace. 'You pinched my bottom last week.'

This time Imi went red.

'Oh *yeah*?' I said.

'I only did it because you *asked* me to,' Imi told Grace. 'You were going on about having buns of steel!'

'Yeah – but the point is, it was just a laugh,' Grace said. 'We didn't end up snogging or anything. It didn't *mean* anything.'

'I know,' replied Imi.

'So what's the big deal with Jit tickling me?' I asked Imi. 'We're all friends, aren't we?'

Imi looked at Jit and then back at me. 'I suppose so,' he said sheepishly.

'*Jit?*' asked Dean, his first serious input into our conversation.

'*What?*' replied Jit.

'We are all mates, *ain't* we?' Dean asked.

'Yeah – I never said we weren't. I just don't like being grabbed up like that.'

'Well in that case – I'm sorry,' said Imi.

Hannah grinned. 'God, that took ages,' she said.

'I'm sorry too,' said Jit. 'For jumping on you and that.'

'*Ahh!* Now, are you going to kiss and make up?' asked Grace.

'I said we were mates,' replied Jit, in disgust. 'But I ain't kissin' his ugly raas!'

'No *way*,' said Imi.

'You should at least shake hands,' suggested Dean.

'Whatever,' said Imi, walking over to Jit and shaking his hand.

'Would have kicked yer ass though,' Jit told him, grinning.

'With *those* skinny arms – doubt it!' replied Imi.

And that was it. They were back to being friends and stopped sulking.

'They threatened something else too, didn't they?' Hannah asked me.

'*What?*' asked Dean.

I nodded. 'Yeah – they said that they'd tell my

parents about Imi and Jit. They said they'd tell Imi's
parents too.'

'*What?*' said Imi, just as Grace's dad came down the
stairs carrying a tray.

'Anyone for drinks?' he asked. He was wearing a
really cool T-shirt that said GOD IS TOO BIG FOR JUST
ONE RELIGION. Above the words were six small circles,
each one carrying the symbol of a different world
religion.

'Er . . . yeah, Dad,' replied Grace. 'Thanks. Just put
them down on the table.'

'Oh, right,' replied Mr Parkhurst, looking upset. 'I
can see I'm not wanted.'

'Dad,' groaned Grace. 'We're having a private conversation.'

Mr Parkhurst smiled. 'A private conversation – all
*six* of you?' he asked.

'Yes,' Grace told him. 'Now *shoo!*'

Mr Parkhurst shrugged and went back upstairs.
'Your dad's T-shirt is wicked,' said Dean, beating me
to the punch. 'Where'd he get it?'

'Dunno,' said Grace. 'And that's beside the point.
We were talking about Justin and Andy.'

'So what do they want?' asked Imi, looking worried.

'Twenty quid – every week.'

'*Nah!* That's just daylight robbery, you get me,' said Jit. 'Were they wearing masks and that?'

'It's not that much money – between us,' said Grace.

I shook my head. 'I'm not giving them anything,' I said.

'But what if they carry out their threat?' asked Imi.

'I'm going to tell my parents the truth before that,' I told them.

'*When?*' asked Jit.

'After the weekend.'

Grace gave me a funny look. 'So what are you going to do about the money this week?' she asked.

'Nothing,' I replied. 'My parents are out all night on Friday, and on Saturday we're all going on a day trip to the seaside.'

'*This* Saturday?' asked Jit.

'Yeah, sorry – I was going to tell you.'

Imi and Grace both pulled a face.

'Is Jit going on this one *too?*' asked Imi.

'Yeah – this is the last one though,' I said. 'I promise. I'll tell them on Sunday. Justin and Andy won't get the chance to get to them before me.'

'Are you sure?' asked Jit, looking concerned.

'Absolutely,' I told him.

Dean stood up and went over to the pool table, picking up the cue ball and turning it in his hand as he spoke.

'We're gonna have to get clever with Justin and Andy,' he said.

'How do you mean?' asked Hannah.

'Well, they've got it in for Suky, me, Jit *and* Imi. We're gonna have to stop them somehow.'

'You could always tell Gussie,' suggested Jit, talking about Dean's older brother.

Dean shook his head.

'Nah – Gussie will go and get all medieval on 'em . . . and get into trouble. It's got to be something clever and slick . . . like in the movies,' he replied.

'And who's going to come up with that plan then?' asked Imi.

'Me,' said Dean. 'Just let me think about it.'

I looked at him and sighed. 'Just don't go getting into trouble. Like I told you – I'll tell my parents at the weekend,' I said.

Dean shook his head again. 'This is going to take

longer than a few days, if I'm honest. It's gonna have to be more of a long-term plan.'

I wondered what he was on about, but left it. An hour later, Imi walked me part of the way home. In bed that night, I thought about how I was going to tell my parents. Which words I was going to use and how I was going to use them. I rehearsed my opening line in my head, over and over, until I fell asleep.

# ELEVEN

I was with Hannah the next morning, walking to registration, when Justin approached me.

'Got my money?' he asked nastily.

'No,' I replied, as Hannah started to look worried.

'Well you've got until tomorrow,' he told me.

'But you said Friday,' I reminded him, trying not to sound like I was bothered, even though I was.

He smirked at me and I wanted to punch him. But I don't do that. I may beat the boys at sports all the time but I'm not violent.

'I changed my mind,' he told me, all self-importantly, as if he was God or something. The ugly, rat-faced gimp.

'Well I haven't got it and I can't get it until Friday so you're gonna have to wait,' I replied, trying this time to sound defiant.

'Thursday – or the parents get a nice anonymous letter or maybe even a knock at the door.'

This time I smirked.

'You turn up at my door and my dad will kick your ass,' I warned.

He thought about it for a moment and I could tell he was concerned. Then he put his rat-face back on and smiled.

'Well then it'll be a letter . . .'

'Why don't you just get lost?' asked Hannah.

'Or go and play with a bottle of Domestos?' I added, feeling more confident. It didn't last long.

Justin scowled and grabbed my bag from me. As I tried to get it off him, he opened it and emptied my stuff all over the floor of the corridor. The other pupils stopped and stared at us. I looked down and saw all my things on the floor. Some little git started laughing behind me.

'*Ehh!* Who comes to school with deodorant?' he squealed.

'From the way you smell – not you, obviously,' snapped Hannah.

The Year Seven lad looked at her in shock, as his friends started laughing at him. I didn't join in. Justin opened my bag wider and then did something really nasty. He cleared his throat and spat into it. Then he threw it back at me and I caught it.

'Tomorrow, or I'll have to get really angry,' he warned, as he walked away.

I dropped my bag and then fell to my knees to collect my things. I had tears in my eyes and when Hannah knelt to help me, I turned my face away.

'He's so gonna get it!' she told me. 'I don't care when and I don't care how – but it's gonna happen.'

I carried on picking up my stuff.

'Are you OK?' she asked.

'No!' I snapped. 'He spat in my bag!'

And then I started crying, which made me even angrier. Hannah picked up the last of my things and helped me into the girls' loo. I put all my stuff on the sink surround and wiped my eyes.

'Want me to clean your bag for you?' asked Hannah.

'No . . . but thanks for offering.'

'I don't mind, honestly,' she added.

I shook my head.

'Just leave it. I don't want it any more – I'll get another,' I told her.

'Well, you're going to need something to carry your things in for the rest of today,' she pointed out.

'Oh . . .' I said. I hadn't even thought about that.

Hannah grinned at me via the mirror that I was staring into. She pulled a plastic bag from her rucksack, and handed it to me.

'I know it's not exactly Louis Vuitton,' she said, 'but it'll do the job.'

I gave her a big hug.

'Whoa, sister . . . a thank you will suffice!' she joked, even though she hugged me back.

'I hate him,' I told her, after I'd let her go.

'You and everyone else in this school.'

I swore a few times.

'Suky! Young ladies don't say things like that,' teased Hannah.

'Stuff that,' I replied. 'Let's get to registration and please don't tell anyone what happened. Please . . .'

'Not even Grace and the lads?' she asked.

'Especially not them. Promise me,' I demanded.

'I promise,' she told me.

I began to put my stuff into the bag and thought about getting some of my big, nasty cousins to beat up Justin for me. But having them kick seven shades of you-know-what out of him wouldn't make me feel better. I'd only be happy if I handled it myself. Or with a little help from my friends. I decided to ask Dean what he had come up with. One way or another, Justin Patel and Andy Stevenson were going to get theirs. Even if it took the rest of the school year for it to happen.

I know it sounds mean, but I only cheered up at lunch time, when Robert and Wesley walked into the room where we make the school newspaper. I'm not a mean person, but somehow talking to Robert and Wesley made me laugh. They were sweet in their own way, but they were also *so* easy to tease. I was with Grace when the two of them arrived. They said that Mr Black wanted us to interview them immediately for the paper. Grace sighed and shook her head.

'Does he realize how much I've got to do?' she joked. 'I've got deadlines pouring out of my nose like watery snot and a print run to deal with and celebrities to slander . . .'

'It'll only take a little while,' said Robert.

'*Only a little while?*' repeated Grace. 'I don't *have* a little while, as you so naively put it. This is the high-pressure world of print media, my lad. No room for sentiment or farting around.'

'But . . .'

I decided that I'd join in too. 'I suppose *I'll* have to do it,' I told them. 'I've got the prime minister on the other line but I'll just have to put him on hold . . .'

'You're doing an article on the *prime minister*?' asked Wesley, looking excited.

'What do *you* think, you silly boy?' asked Grace.

'We're teasing you,' I told them, as Wesley went bright red. He pushed his glasses up on the bridge of his nose.

'Oh – I see,' said Robert, smiling. 'Humour . . . something which pervades the series of novels we adore.'

Grace tried to stop herself laughing but only managed it by kicking her right shin with her left foot.

'*OWWW!*'

'Is something the matter, Grace?' asked Robert, looking very concerned.

'Oh – it's nothing,' Grace told him. 'Just a little involuntary twitch. Runs in the family, I'm afraid.'

'My family has a history of mild insanity,' offered Wesley.

'*Really?*' I asked, stepping on my own toe to stop the laughter.

'Yes – it's very strange. Seems to appear at random,' he continued.

'That's all well and good, Mr Magoogan,' said Robert, trying to show authority, 'but we are here to be interviewed about chess.'

'*Exactly*,' agreed Grace. 'How lovely that we think along the same lines, Robert.'

I knew that she was still teasing, but Robert has a massive crush on Grace and he smiled so broadly that I thought he might swallow his own ears.

'Erm ... I – I ... yes ... er ...' he stammered, which was like his default setting whenever Grace was nice to him.

Grace stood up and went over to him, leaning in to his left ear.

'So, what can I help you with?' she whispered.

Robert pulled back slightly and almost giggled.

'Erm ... er ... haha ...' he mumbled.

'Perhaps we could start with a little chat about your interests?' I suggested.

'What a wonderful idea,' agreed Grace, still close enough to Robert that he could feel her breath against his skin. He went the same colour as Wesley; I could have sworn that I saw steam coming from his ears too. Well, OK – maybe I didn't.

'I was thinking about that series you mentioned – *The Dark World of Lazywitch*?' I said.

Robert cleared his throat. 'I think you'll find that it's called *The Dark Lord of Hazelwitch*,' he corrected.

'Yeah – that,' I continued. It wasn't that I didn't know what the series was called – you couldn't get away from the silly books – I just wanted Robert and Wesley to get excited about them and, true to form, they did.

'We're just re-reading the first seven books,' Wesley informed us. 'Ready for the sequels to appear on Christmas Eve.'

'You mentioned that a few days ago,' I said. 'What's that all about?'

'Well,' replied Robert, 'there are two sequels because Princess Wondlebarn, the heroine, has had to travel back in time to before her own birth to save the people of Hazelwitch from Gerafaggan. He's the Dark Lord—'

'Why does the Princess have to travel back in time? Isn't there a knight in shining armour to rescue her from the drudgery of her existence and whisk her away to somewhere nice with shops?' asked Grace.

Wesley smiled. Then he unleashed a wave of information at us.

'There are rumours that she'll meet her prince in the past but they've not been verified by the author. What's happened is this – Tar, the giant rat and former friend of the Royal House of Hazelwitch, has been turned to the Dark Way by the evil Lord Gerafaggan. He has stolen the Ancient Flute of Kings and given it to the Dark Lord. Now the Dark Lord—'

'Is Tar actually *rat* spelled backwards?' asked Grace.

'Yes – but do let me finish,' replied Wesley, the closest I'd ever seen him to being annoyed.

Obviously Hazelwitch fans were not to be trifled with, not where their precious series was concerned. Grace said '*Ooh*' and continued listening.

'The Dark Lord is aware of the power vested in the Princess from the Stones of Gajamash and he has spirited the Ancient Flute away to the distant past to keep her from it. If the Princess can get the flute, then she can find all the Gajamash Stones, bring them together and end the tyranny of the Dark Lord. But she has to find the flute first and that's where Pitchy-Patchy comes in . . .'

'Who?' I asked.

'Pitchy-Patchy. He's a magical being from the Time Beyond Time When All Things Were Equal. Equilibrium Time, it's called. Anyway, he has a magic rod, which he hides under his skirts—'

'Wesley – are you being *rude*?' asked Grace.

'No – why ever would you ask me that?' he replied, looking embarrassed.

'Well a magic *rod* – *under* his skirts – it all sounds a bit rude to me,' Grace told him.

'Very rude,' I said.

'*Ruder* than rude,' added Grace.

'Like the rudest thing you've ever heard but ten times worse . . .' I continued.

'*So* rude that if the biggest piece of rude in the *whole* world came and farted in your face, it couldn't be ruder . . .' finished Grace.

'Oh, do let him continue,' said Robert.

Wesley cleared his throat, pushed his glasses back up the bridge of his nose, and finished his outline of the Hazelwitch series so far.

'So, Pitchy-Patchy has been sent by the God of Gajamash to help the Princess in her quest, and he's going to use his magic rod to take her back into the past. That's where the story has got to, thus far.'

I looked at him and wondered how it took seven books to tell the story he had just outlined. I asked him but Robert decided it was his turn to speak.

'Oh, there *are* other strands to the tale, but that's the *main* one. In fact there is a wonderful secondary plot featuring the Bongo Monkey, but that's something else entirely—'

'Oh *damn*!' said Grace. 'Would you look at the time. I must be going.'

'Where are *you* going?' I asked her.

'To eat something . . . I said I'd meet Hannah in the dining hall.'

I groaned. 'But why didn't you eat when I did?' I asked.

'Wasn't hungry,' she replied, grinning slyly. 'Thank God!'

'Great!' I said, as she grabbed her stuff and walked out of the classroom.

Robert and Wesley turned to me with mad grins on their faces, like evil scientists who had just found a new specimen to play with.

'Right,' I told them loudly. 'Let's get on with this interview, then . . .'

'Yes,' replied Robert. 'Perhaps we could tell you the

story of Bongo Monkey and the search for the Land of—'

'Oh, God!' I groaned, as Wesley pushed his glasses back up his face for the third time.

# TWELVE

Things weren't so funny when I finished school for the day. The first sign was Jit, who ran past me as I was making my way out of school with Imi. Justin, with Dean following close behind, was chasing him.

'Oh, what now?' I asked.

'Dunno,' said Imi, 'but we'd better go and see.'

*Here we go again*, I thought as I followed Imi.

We found Jit sitting on the tennis court steps, bleeding from a cut lip and being calmed down by Dean. Again.

'Leave it, bro . . . they'll just batter you again,' Dean was saying as we joined them.

'I don't *care*!' shouted Jit. 'I'm gonna kill that Justin!'

'What happened?' I asked.

'Justin beat him up,' Dean told me. 'Something about making him regret coming to school every day.'

'He wants revenge for his cousin,' Jit added.

'What *revenge?*' I asked. 'You didn't do anything to Jason.'

Dean looked away.

'Dean's brother battered him over them dodgy phones,' Jit told me, talking about an incident from a few weeks earlier.

'But didn't Jason get kicked out for beating up someone else?' asked Imi.

'Yeah, he did, but he told Justin about me and Dean,' replied Jit.

Imi nodded.

'And now he's after both of us,' said Dean. 'Although the ugly tosser's only picking on Jit.'

'Have you come up with anything to stop him?' I asked.

'Not yet,' he replied. 'But give me time.'

'Jit doesn't look like he's got any time,' I pointed out.

Jit stood up and wiped the blood from his mouth onto his sleeve. 'Don't worry about me,' he said, acting all hard. 'I've been hit harder than that before.'

'That's *not* the point,' I told him. 'You shouldn't *have* to get beaten up all the time.'

Dean looked at me. 'Who's gonna stop it?' he asked.

'Just tell your brother,' suggested Imi.

'I can't,' said Dean. 'He'll get into trouble.'

'So what are we gonna do?' I asked.

'Leave it with me, like I said,' replied Dean.

I was about to say something else when Grace and Hannah ran over to us. I thought that they were concerned about Jit but I was wrong. They'd opened their big mouths once too often.

'He overheard us,' said Grace, trying to get her breath back.

'*Who?*' asked Dean.

'The Skunk!' panted Hannah.

'*Andy?*' said Imi.

They both nodded. Hannah wouldn't look me in the eye.

'What do you *mean* he overheard?' I asked. '*What* did he hear?'

Grace looked at her feet, waiting for Hannah to speak. Hannah said nothing.

'*Well?*'

'Oh all right then!' replied Grace. 'But it wasn't our fault, OK. We didn't know he was there.'

'Will you just tell us what happened?' I asked, getting wound up.

'We were standing by the entrance to the art department, talking about what you said,' began Grace. 'About telling your parents before Justin and Andy could get to them.'

'Oh *no!*'

'And Andy just appeared from nowhere,' added Hannah.

'You *told* them?' I said, getting angry.

'*No!*' snapped Grace. 'We were just talking. How were we supposed to know that he was listening to us?'

I shook my head.

'You know what it's like in this school. Even the walls gossip.'

'We're sorry,' said Hannah.

'Yeah – we didn't mean it,' added Grace, looking tearful.

'That's a major help – a *huge*, great help!' I snapped, before feeling bad.

'*What* did he hear?' asked Dean.

'We were talking about how brave Suky was being for refusing to give them her money and how she was going to tell her parents about Imi and Jit; and I was saying that it was about time and . . .' said Grace.

'And he heard all of it?' I asked.

'I think so,' admitted Grace. 'I'm so sorry.'

I told her that it wasn't their fault. They didn't know that Skunk Boy was hiding nearby. But it did give me a problem. A big one. Jit pointed it out.

'If they know that you ain't gonna pay them tomorrow, then what have they got to lose?' he asked me.

'I was just thinking the same thing,' agreed Imi.

'They ain't got no reason not to tell your parents now, have they?' Jit added.

'I know,' I replied.

'And while we been standin' around here talking about it,' said Dean, 'I bet they're already on a bus headin' for your parents' house.'

'Oh crap!' I said.

'No need for that kind of language, Miss Kaur,' I heard a familiar voice say behind us. It was Mr Herbert.

'No need for that *face* either,' mumbled Dean.

'I *beg* your pardon?' asked Herbert.

'Nuttin',' replied Dean. 'I wasn't talkin' to you. School's finished so you ain't got no hold over what I say anyhow.'

'Yeah, if I was you, I'd run along,' added Jit, grinning.

'This *is* still school property!' Herbert shouted.

'See ya!' Dean said casually.

We walked out of school and went to get the bus. Jit, Dean and Hannah, who lived on a completely different bus route, waited with me, Imi and Grace.

'Are you coming too?' asked Grace.

'*Yeah!*' said Hannah. 'We don't wanna miss out on all the fun.'

I glared at her.

'Sorry, Suky,' she replied, looking slightly ashamed. There was nothing funny about my problem. Nothing at all.

My parents were both in when I got back, with the gang in tow.

'Blimey,' said my dad, when he saw us all. 'We havin' a party?'

'We just wanted to talk about a project we're all doing together,' I lied.

'All of you?' he asked.

'Yes, Mr Singh,' said Grace.

'And how are your parents, Grace?' asked my dad.

'Cool,' she replied.

I looked at my mum, who half smiled. She looked tired.

'Has anyone called for me?' I asked her.

'Er . . . not that I know of,' she replied. 'Not since I've been at home anyway.'

'What about since then?' I asked.

'No – why were you *expecting* someone?'

'No . . . well just these two lads from school.'

My dad shook his head.

'More project members?' he asked.

'Er . . . yeah.'

'I've been back since two,' he told me. 'No one's called round at all.'

I looked at Hannah and Grace in turn, and they both looked away.

'Anything in the post?' I asked my mum.

'Usual stuff. Are you expecting something?'

I nodded. 'From a pen pal,' I lied.

'What pen pal?' she asked, getting up from the kitchen table to put her coffee mug on the side.

'Just this girl I speak to on the net,' I said, wondering how I found it so easy to lie.

'Oh – right. First *I've* heard of it.'

'It's a teenager thing,' said my dad. 'Secrets . . .'

He winked at me, and for a second I thought that he knew, but he didn't. How could he have known when Justin and Andy hadn't been round?

My mum smiled at my friends.

'I suppose you lot'll be going upstairs to Suky's room?' she asked.

'Yeah,' said Hannah. 'Lots of work to do.'

'Well you'll be wanting drinks, then,' replied my mum.

She looked at Jit. 'Can you help me with the drinks, Imtiaz?' she asked, yawning.

Jit shot me a quick look and then corrected her.

'You mean Jit?' he said.

'Oh my God!' replied my mum. 'I'm doing far too many hours at work. I'm sorry, Jit.'

'No worries,' replied Jit.

'So,' she said, smiling at Imi and Jit. 'Perhaps you can *both* help?'

'Of course . . . Mrs . . . er . . .' began Imi.

'Tina, please, Imtiaz. I'm not used to all that formal nonsense. By the way, I spoke to your mum last night.'

'Oh – she didn't say,' said Imi.

'Well, we're having another baby,' she said, without any thought to my feelings at all. Talk about embarrassment. It was one thing to get yourself pregnant when you're old. It was another thing entirely to heap shame upon your teenage daughter too.

'And I wanted to talk to her about it,' added my mum. 'Women's stuff, you know . . .'

'*MUM!*' I shouted.

'Oh grow up, Suky . . . people have babies all the time.'

'We're *going* up to my room now,' I told her, relieved that she didn't know anything about what was going on with me, Imi and Jit.

'Would you like some sandwiches?' she asked us.

Dean looked at me, then at Jit, and finally he nodded.

'Yeah! I'm starvin'!' he told my mum.

'Ham and cheese all right for everyone?' she asked.

'Er . . . not for me,' said Imi.

My mum smiled at him.

'I know that. I used to make your packed lunches when you were little – *remember*? Your mum and I used to take turns.'

'I'm a vegetarian,' added Grace. 'Hannah is too.'

Hannah pinched Grace on the arm.

'I'll have the ham,' she told my mum.

'But I thought you were a veggie?' moaned Grace.

Hannah grinned, as we walked up to my room.

'I *was*,' she replied. 'And then my mum cooked a big, fat steak one day and I couldn't resist!'

'You stinky, smelly, *dirty* girl . . .' said Grace.

# THIRTEEN

I was dreading school the next morning and prayed that I didn't bump into Justin or Andy. As I got off the bus I looked around to make sure that they weren't waiting for me and then I hurried into school. The corridors were busy with pupils. I kept an eye out for Andy's strange hair, but I didn't see him or Justin. By the time I sat down in my form room, I was out of breath.

'What's up with *you*?' asked Puspha, one of the girls in my class.

'Nothing,' I replied.

'You're all out of breath,' added another girl called Heather.

'No, I'm not,' I lied, wondering where my friends were.

Heather gave me a funny look and then started asking me about the school paper. Whilst I was talking to her, Grace and Hannah walked in, with Imi right behind them.

'You OK?' asked Hannah.

'Yeah – why *shouldn't* I be?'

'We thought you might have bumped into Justin and Andy,' said Imi.

'I haven't seen them at all,' I replied. 'It's probably too early for them anyway.'

Grace sat down next to me and put her bag on the table.

'I hope they don't go after Jit again,' she said.

'Well, if he told the teachers what they're up to, they might stop,' I pointed out.

'So are you going to the seaside on Saturday?' she asked.

'Yeah – we're leaving really early in the morning.'

Hannah grinned.

'But it's October,' she said. 'It'll be freezing!'

I shrugged. 'That's my dad for you,' I told her. 'Weirdo . . .'

'He'll probably take you to the North Pole next summer,' teased Grace.

'Knowing him, you're probably right,' I said.

Mrs Dooher walked in with a hamster cage, covered in dark blue cloth, and put it down on her desk.

'What's *that*, miss?' asked Heather.

'It's a cage,' replied Mrs Dooher drily. 'What does it look like?'

'Yeah, but what's in it?' said Dilip.

'A rat,' Mrs Dooher told him.

'*EHHHHHHHH!*' came a loud shout from half the classroom.

'Oh, do shut up!' Mrs Dooher half shouted. 'It's not a wild rat . . . it's a pet.'

'*Nah!* What kind of weirdo keeps a rat as a pet?' asked Marco.

'My daughters,' admitted Mrs Dooher.

'Man, that's just sick!' said Milorad.

'No it isn't,' replied Grace. 'What's the *difference* between a rat and a hamster? Or a guinea pig?'

'Plenty,' said Marco.

'No there *isn't*,' protested Grace. 'And besides, they're all pointless. All they do is stuff their faces, poo and run around on wheels all day.'

'Do they eat their poo too, like rabbits?' asked Hannah.

'I'm not sure,' replied Mrs Dooher. 'I'll have to ask my daughters.'

Marco stood up and walked over to the cage. He lifted the cloth and a little snout poked out from between the bars, shocking him.

'*AHH!*' he screamed.

'You big baby!' laughed Hannah.

'*No!* I wasn't scared,' he lied.

'Yes you were!' said Dilip. 'You're just *gay*, you are!'

'*DILIP!*'

The whole class stopped what they were doing and looked at Mrs Dooher in awe. She had never really raised her voice before and we were all shocked. Especially Dilip. You could have driven a bus into his gob.

'We don't use racist, sexist or homophobic language in this school – do you understand?'

'But I didn't, miss,' whined Dilip. 'I only called him gay . . .'

'That *is* homophobic, you pea brain,' I heard Dean say from the doorway. Jit was standing next to him. I smiled at them both.

'*No!* I'm not homo . . .!' protested Dilip.

'Dilip,' said Mrs Dooher in her usual voice. 'You were saying Marco was gay and implying that that is somehow wrong. I won't allow that. You're entitled to your opinion, but when it's as nasty as that, kindly keep it to yourself. Understand?'

Dilip sighed.

'Yes, miss. But I didn't mean it . . . I'm not homoph . . . ph . . . that thing.'

'I'm glad to hear it,' said Mrs Dooher.

'So, why *have* you brought your daughters' pet to school?' asked Hannah.

'Well – originally there were two,' she told us all. 'Mop and Bucket. But Mop died and my daughters couldn't bear to keep Bucket on his own.'

'How did he die?' asked Milorad.

Mrs Dooher pulled a strange face, like she was trying not to grin. It didn't work.

'My eldest daughter, Nancy—' she began.

'Is she *fit*, miss?' asked Dilip.

'Who?'

'Your daughter,' he explained.

'Oh, shut up, Dilip,' replied Mrs Dooher. 'Anyway, Nancy let him out of the cage and Mop ran out of the room. He went and hid in the cellar, and the other day my husband went down to get a bottle of wine . . .'

'And found him *dead*?' asked Marco excitedly.

'Er . . . no. Not exactly,' she said. 'Fran – that's my husband – he pulled out a bottle of wine and it slipped from his hands, and just at that moment poor Mop poked his head out from under the wine rack.'

She tried really hard not to laugh but it was no use. She cracked up and had trouble finishing the story.

'. . . He . . . he . . . said that the bottle b . . . b . . . bounced off the poor little thing's head! Squashed it flat!'

Mrs Dooher let out a shriek of laughter and we all followed. When she'd calmed herself down, she told us the rest.

'So anyway, Katie – that's my youngest – and Nancy agreed to let your class take care of Bucket, and here he is.'

She lifted the cloth off the cage. Heather screamed. Dilip giggled and Marco fainted. I looked at Jit whilst all this was happening and asked him about Saturday.

'I'm sorted,' he told me. 'My mum's going to drop me off round the corner from yours, early.'

'Why not at the door?' I asked.

'*DOH!* What if your dad sees her? Starts asking her questions?'

'Oh yeah,' I said, as Mrs Dooher tried to revive Marco. The big wuss.

I didn't see Justin or Andy at all during school. On

my way home, I pointed it out to Grace and Imi.

'Don't you think it's a bit weird?' I said.

'Maybe they were just bunking off?' suggested Grace.

'On the day that they wanted me to give them money? I doubt it,' I replied.

'Well, they did overhear Grace and Hannah saying that you wouldn't do that,' said Imi.

'No – that doesn't make sense either,' I replied.

Then I had a terrible thought.

'What if they went round to my house today?'

'Oh,' said Imi.

'Ploppy pants!' added Grace.

'What if my parents are waiting for me right now – ready to batter me for lying to them? I think I'm going to be sick,' I said.

'You don't even know that's what's happened,' replied Grace, trying to reassure me.

'I don't know that it hasn't either,' I pointed out.

When I got in my parents *were* waiting for me but they didn't let rip when I walked into the kitchen. Instead they asked me if I'd had a good day at school. I said that I had and then my dad showed me a phone bill.

'You've been doing a lot of texting,' he said.

'Huh?'

'The phone bill is huge,' explained my mum.

'Oh – right,' I replied, calming down.

My phone is on the same contract as my parents' and I have a monthly limit that I'm not supposed to go over.

'*I'm* not going to pay for your excessive phone use,' said my dad, only he didn't seem that angry. In fact he seemed like he was trying not to laugh or something.

'No matter *how* much you text Jit,' said my mum. 'That's who it is, isn't it?'

'Yeah,' I said.

'But you see him all day, every day at school,' added my dad. 'How much can you possibly have to talk about?'

I grinned at him. 'It's a teenage thing,' I said. 'You wouldn't understand, you old git.'

'Well the phone bill is a *money* thing. Maybe if you use *your* pocket money to pay for *your* overspend – you'll understand, you *young* git,' he replied.

'But, Dad!'

'No arguments, Suky,' said my mum. 'After this

weekend, your pocket money goes towards paying the bill . . . OK?'

I groaned.

'Whatever . . .'

'No letters today,' my dad told me.

'What?'

'No letters . . . you were expecting one from your pen pal?'

'Oh yeah . . . er . . . I'll e-mail her to find out what happened to it,' I told him.

'Funny girl,' said my mum. 'You'll be even worse when the baby is born . . . acting jealous and stuff.'

'Won't,' I said. 'I'm not a kid!'

My gran walked in with a cup of tea in her hands. She was spilling it everywhere.

'Careful, Mum,' my dad said to her in Punjabi.

'Oh go and poke out your own eyes,' she replied.

'Told!' I teased him, in English.

'And you can shut up too, you fat dog!' said my gran.

I looked at my mum and dad, who started to crease up with laughter.

'You horrible old gits!' I said angrily, stomping off to my room.

# FOURTEEN

Justin and Andy were standing by the bus stop after school the next day, picking on a load of Year Sevens. I saw them from about fifty metres away and started to slow down. Grace, who was walking with me, saw them too.

'Oh great! That's all we need after a whole afternoon of Maths and Science,' she moaned.

'What do we do?' I asked.

Grace shrugged. 'Nothing . . . we're going to get the bus and if they try and mess us about, I'll karate-chop them – *yee-hah*!'

She kicked out her left leg and nearly went flying in the process.

'Oh, be serious, Grace,' I told her.

'Well, we can't let them stop us from catching our bus – that would just be silly.'

'So, what do we do?' I asked.

'Simple – ignore them,' she replied.

That was easy to say. It proved impossible to do, though. When we reached the bus stop, Andy was picking his nose and wiping what he found up his flared, hairy nostrils on a lad standing in front of him.

'*Yuk!*' said Grace, turning up her own nose. 'He's nasty.'

Andy did the same thing about three more times and then he saw us.

'Ah . . . it's the ugly twins,' he smirked.

Justin, who had another Year Seven by his ears, turned round and saw us too. He let the lad go and the poor kid ran off crying. Justin pulled out his mobile phone and videoed him running. Then he turned it towards me and Grace.

'So, you think you don't have to pay us?' he said to me, in a stupid posh accent.

'Get lost!' I replied, praying for the bus to turn up.

'Well, that's fine,' he told me. 'Splendid, in fact.'

'*Huh?*' I said, shocked.

'I admire your bravery in standing up to the school bully,' he continued.

Andy coughed.

'I'm sorry – did I say bully? I meant *bullies . . .*' corrected Justin.

He grinned at me, showing his manky, yellow teeth. They looked like they'd never been cleaned.

'After all,' he said, 'it takes *two* to tango . . .'

'I'm sorry?' I asked.

'No need to be sorry,' said Andy. 'Just think about it.' He was trying to copy Justin's terrible accent and doing even worse.

I looked at Grace. She shrugged and put an index finger to her right temple, twirling it.

'*Loco* . . .' she whispered.

'Did you understand me?' asked Justin.

'Are you on drugs?' I asked.

Justin grinned again. 'Only you . . .' He smirked. 'Two to tango . . . remember that. Think about it . . . ta-ra!'

And with that, he grabbed Andy by the shoulder and the two of them walked off.

'That was surreal,' said Grace.

'What does that mean?'

Grace shrugged. 'My mum says it all the time, when weird stuff happens.'

'Which is all the time in your house.'

'Yep!'

I watched the two bullies walking away and asked

Grace if I was going mad. 'I think he just kind of asked me out,' I said, shocked at what my own voice was saying.

'*No!* Well, OK . . . maybe,' she replied.

'He said that he was smiling because of me, and then he kept saying it takes two to tango . . . and to *think* about it. Think about *what*?'

Grace shrugged again.

'But he could have meant *anything*,' she said.

'Yeah, but all the same.'

'It takes two *what* to tango, anyway?' she asked. 'Elephants? *Monkeys*?'

'That was so freaky,' I replied.

'I can see how it would be,' said Grace. 'Two elephants doing the tango. They'd need enormous dresses and reinforced high-heels too . . .'

The bus appeared in my line of vision just as she'd replied, saving me from even more weirdness.

Until I got home, that is. Once again my parents were in the kitchen, snogging, when I walked in.

'Will you stop it!' I shouted when I saw them. 'That's just *disgusting*!'

'Oh shut up, you little witch!' replied my mum, as

my dad turned purple and walked out of the kitchen.

'Oh my God!'

'*Well* . . . you're like a forty-year-old in a teenager's body. Why don't you take a chill pill?'

I raised an eyebrow.

'*OK* – snog all you like but whatever you do – *don't* say *that* in front of my friends *ever* – OK?' I told her.

'Say *what*?'

'*Chill pill* – it's just *wrong*!'

My mum shook her head and sat down at the table.

'Imi rang for you . . .'

'When?' I asked.

'About five minutes ago,' she replied.

'What did he say?'

'Nothing much. Just to call him back when you got home.'

I wondered why he hadn't called me on my mobile.

'Must have been about the project,' I told her.

'You'll find out if you call him back,' she suggested, with added sarcasm.

'No need to be rude, is there?' I said, pulling my mobile out of my bag.

I found Imi's number and pressed the green dial button. Nothing happened. I hit cancel and then tried again. And again. And again. Still nothing.

'Bloody thing!' I shouted. 'It hasn't got a signal.'

My mum shook her head.

'I think you'll find it hasn't got a line,' she explained.

'What?'

'Your dad had it cut off temporarily.'

'That's not fair!' I shouted. 'I *need* this phone. What if I lose my number as well – that's just mean!'

'You won't lose the number. Your dad already checked that out. But you *will* pay back the money you owe. Maybe we'll change our minds after that.'

I sat down at the table.

'You were in on it too?' I asked.

'Yes. You owe twenty pounds on top of what your dad pays monthly. I mean – who were you calling – Santa Claus, in Lapland?'

I shrugged.

'Only Jit – and my other friends,' I said quietly.

'Tough!' she replied, smiling slightly. The freak.

'I'd better use the landline,' I told her.

'Only if you're quick. And I mean super-quick!'

'*Whatever!*' I snapped, picking up the home phone and dialling.

Mrs Dhondy picked up the phone and I asked her if Imi was there.

'Oh, no, Suky. He's out with his dad. Won't be back until *very* late.'

'Can I leave him a message in that case?' I asked.

'Of course you can,' she told me.

'Can you ask him to call me as soon as he gets this message. Thank you.'

'You're welcome. Have fun at the seaside tomorrow,' said Mrs Dhondy before hanging up.

I turned to my mum.

'Did he say what he wanted?' I asked.

'*Who?*' she asked, being all vague.

'Imtiaz . . .'

'No – just something about calling him.'

'Nothing else?'

My mum shook her head.

'No. Now can you get a pen and a bit of paper please?' she asked.

'Why – you going to give me a *test*?' I replied.

'Uh-uh. We're going shopping,' she told me.

# FIFTEEN

I opened the door to Jit the next morning and yawned at him.

'Hello to you too,' he said, grinning.

'How can you be so *awake*?' I asked him. 'It's only seven a.m.'

'So?'

'*So* – you can't even make it to school for *nine* most mornings and here you are at seven a.m., looking all awake and *smiling*.'

Jit grinned. 'Maybe I'm excited about the trip?' he suggested.

'*Why?*'

'I've never been to the seaside before,' he admitted.

'Huh?'

'*Honest*. I've never seen the sea. Well, I *have*, but only in films and on the telly.'

I ushered him into the living room. 'You're lying . . .

you must have seen it . . . not even when you were a little kid?'

He shook his head. 'I've never really been on holiday. My mum used to take me to London when I was younger – to go and look at the sights and that; but that's all,' he said.

'Oh,' I replied, not knowing what to say. It was too early in the morning anyway.

'I'm just going to get my stuff together,' I told him.

'Better get a coat too,' he told me. 'It ain't exactly warm out there.'

I groaned and left him in the room on his own for a few minutes. When I returned, he was sitting on the sofa, pressed against one arm, as though he was trying to hide. My gran was sitting almost on top of him, asking him questions in Punjabi.

'Gran – leave him alone.'

She looked at me and started to speak, only I couldn't understand a word she was saying because she didn't have her teeth in. Jit actually looked scared but calmed down when she got up and walked out of the room.

'Having fun?' I teased.

'It's going to be like this all day,' he said.

'What was she saying?' I asked.

'I dunno. All I could see was her gums. Getting closer and closer. And she kept on farting – it was nasty!'

'Oh, she's harmless really,' I told him.

'*What?* She'd scare vampires!'

I laughed. 'She probably would too.'

I told him to come into the kitchen where my mum was making sandwiches, and to pick out the ones he wanted, so that he didn't end up with food he disliked. When my mum saw him she grinned broadly.

'Hello, Jit!' she said.

'Hi . . .'

'What do you like then – in your sandwiches, I mean?'

'Er . . . I'm not that fussy really, Mrs . . .'

'Tina, please . . .' my mum told him.

'Tina.'

'I've got chicken and bacon in mayo, tuna mayo, ham, chicken, cheese and salad. And there's cold tandoori chicken pieces, barbecue wings, samosas and pakora too.'

Jit looked at the mountain of food in the

kitchen. 'That's a *lot* of food,' he said.

'Oh, didn't Suky tell you. Her uncle Mandeep and his family are coming too.'

Jit shot me a look and then smiled at my mum.

'Oh, yeah,' he said. 'I totally forgot.'

'Well – what do you *like*?' continued my mum.

'Well *my* mum made me some too, but she didn't make much, so can I have the chicken and bacon ones please?'

My mum smiled even wider.

'Growing boy like you needs to eat. Don't worry – I'll put a good selection together for you.'

I heard my dad come stomping down the stairs and went out into the hallway.

'You want me to go and fetch the lad?' he asked, swinging his keys in his hand.

'He's already here,' I told him.

'*Already?* He's a good lad, that Jit.'

'He's in the kitchen.'

My dad walked past me and into the kitchen. He saw all the food on the table, grabbed a pakora, coated it in mayonnaise and stuffed it into his gob. When he'd swallowed it, he asked Jit who'd dropped him off.

'My mum,' said Jit.

'And she didn't come and say *hello*?' asked my mum. 'You should have asked her in. I'm *dying* to meet her.'

Jit started going red so I stepped in.

'I'm sure you'll meet his parents soon enough,' I said. 'When they're good and ready. Not everyone is as forward as you two, you know.'

'But she could have just popped her head in the door and said hello,' suggested my mum.

'Next time,' said Jit. 'I'll ask her.'

My mum looked at my dad and then carried on making sandwiches, piles of them.

'You nearly done, Sweets?' asked my dad.

'Just about,' she replied.

'What time is Uncle Mandeep getting here?' I asked, hoping that we could off-load my gran on him.

'He's not,' replied my dad. 'Meeting us down there instead.'

'Oh,' I said.

Jit was eyeing the food so I asked him if he'd had any breakfast.

'Er . . . no – I don't normally eat breakfast.'

On hearing that, my mum started fussing about how young people didn't look after themselves enough and she almost force-fed Jit a load of samosas and chicken. He didn't complain though, piling his way through it all. I don't know where he puts it – he's so skinny.

'Is Rita bringing food too?' asked my dad, talking about my aunt.

'I think so – but don't worry . . . it's going to be a long day and we'll get through it,' she replied, winking at him.

'You mean Dad will,' I said, laughing. 'Greedy fat boy really loves his food!'

'You cheeky cow!' he said, patting his belly. 'All bought and paid for, this.'

We were ready to go about fifteen minutes later and I asked Jit if he needed anything.

'I'm OK,' he said.

'I've got some books and stuff.'

He shrugged. 'I've got one book you'll love,' I added.

'I ain't really into books and that,' he said.

'Trust me,' I told him. 'This one I'm on about is wicked. It's about normal kids . . . just like us.'

'Really?' he asked.

I nodded. 'It's by some guy that used to go to our school as well.'

'Nah!'

'Yeah . . . I've got it in one of my bags.'

I had three bags with me. A big one for my extra clothes and toiletries, a medium one to hold my books and magazines and stuff; and a smaller one, which was my carry bag. A girl's gotta be prepared. I pulled out the book and gave it to him. He started by looking at the colourful cover and then read the blurb on the back. By the time I had closed my bag, he was on page one.

'See?'

'Sounds OK,' he told me. 'It's got swearing and sex on the first page too!'

'It's cool – my mum bought it for me.'

Jit closed the book and told me he'd read some more on the journey.

'How long does it take?' he asked me.

'Two hours . . . maybe three. Depends on the traffic.'

My dad finished loading the people carrier and told us to get in. Then he asked if I had seen my gran. I shrugged.

'Silly old goat,' he mumbled.

She emerged from her little granny annexe about five minutes later, still not wearing her teeth. When my dad asked her where they were, she fished them out of an old, battered handbag and showed them to him. He groaned and told her to put them in, which she did, and she only swore at him once. I smiled at Jit, as my gran got in. She sat in the middle row of seats and Jit and me sat in the back.

'Right!' said my dad, as my mum climbed aboard. 'Let's go!'

My gran called him a slimy, rancid toad, I think, and then she farted.

# SIXTEEN

We stopped at a service station about two hours after leaving home. Jit had fallen asleep with the book that I'd given him open on his lap. I woke him up and asked him if he needed the loo.

'Wha'?'

'We've stopped at the services,' I said.

'Oh – right. Sorry I fell asleep,' he said, gathering himself together.

'No problem. You didn't miss much.'

'What were you doing?' he asked.

'Trying to ignore my gran and wondering why the roads are so boring.'

'Was she on one, yeah?'

'Just a bit,' I replied, getting out of the car.

Jit followed and stretched his arms, yawning. 'Where are we?' he asked.

'Dunno . . .'

'About an hour from the coast,' said my dad. 'I can smell the sea already.'

All *I* could smell was sewage works, although that might have been my gran, who had farted for the entire two hours. But it wasn't her fault. The poor woman had a wind problem. My dad asked us if we wanted drinks and then set off with my mum and my gran towards the shops. I told Jit I was going to the loo.

'I'll meet you outside,' he said. 'I need to go too.'

The service station was packed with people but none of them looked very happy. I suppose it was because it was such a horrible day, windy with little bits of rain. The clouds were dark grey too. Not exactly the best day to go to the coast. Not that it had bothered my dad. When I'd brought it up on the journey, he'd just smiled and gone on about the bracing morning air and how the town we were going to had old smugglers' caves that you could visit.

'It's a great place,' he'd told me.

'Better be,' I'd replied.

Now, as I stood in the foyer, looking for the toilets, I prayed for a bit of sunshine. An old man walked past me and smiled.

'Cheer up, love – it might never happen,' he said, all breezily.

I smiled back and wondered what might not happen and then I saw the sign for the ladies.

I rejoined Jit five minutes later and we walked around the shops, going in and out, looking at things aimlessly.

'My mum gave me some spending money,' he told me. 'She never gives me money normally.'

'You won't need it,' I told him.

'Why?'

'My dad won't let you pay for anything.'

He shook his head. 'I'm not scrounging off your dad,' he told me. 'No way!'

I laughed. 'It's not scrounging, you fool. He's just got this Punjabi thing about taking guests anywhere. You're a guest, so you don't pay. For anything . . .'

Jit thought about it for a moment as we stood in front of a magazine rack and then he grinned.

'What if I see a Ferrari that I want?'

I grinned back. 'You wish!'

'Well, I'm gonna get my mum something and he's not paying for that,' he added.

Jit has had a hard life and I knew that his mum was

poor. My parents were rich and I tried to think of something to say that wouldn't hurt his feelings. But in the end I was just honest.

'Don't tell him, then,' I suggested. 'Because he will pay for it if he sees you.'

Jit nodded and picked up a magazine with a semi-naked model on the front.

'Put that down – you dirty young man!' I shouted.

Jit looked around and saw people staring. He dropped the magazine and walked away, followed by me, laughing my head off.

'That wasn't fair,' he said.

'Oh – I was only kidding. You would have laughed if Grace had done it,' I replied.

'No I wouldn't!' he protested.

I smiled at him. 'Come on, Jit. I reckon we know each other quite well now. You can admit that you fancy Grace . . . I won't tell.'

Jit shrugged. 'Even if I did,' he told me, 'she wouldn't go out with me. Me and her – we're too different.'

'Says who?' I asked.

'It's just the way it is,' he replied.

'She fancies you.'

'Huh?' He looked shocked.

'Of course she does . . . look at how she's been funny about you and me pretending.'

Jit thought for a moment. 'Did she *tell* you that she liked me?' he asked.

'Not in so many words. Me and Hannah just guessed.'

'So you don't really know then?'

'Jit! Everyone knows . . .'

He looked away, embarrassed.

'OK then,' I said to him. 'If she did like you – would you go out with her?'

'That ain't happenin',' he said, trying to deflect the question.

'But if it did . . . just pretend.'

'I dunno,' he replied. 'Probably, yeah.'

I had a brainwave.

'Do you want me to find out for you?' I asked.

'NO!' he said quickly.

'I won't make it obvious.'

'Just forget about it,' he told me, walking off towards the food court.

I followed him, only to find my parents looking worried.

'Your gran's gone walkabout,' said my mum.

'What?'

'We can't find her.'

'Well, she can't have got very far,' said Jit. 'It's not that big a place.'

My dad looked around and then suggested we split up to see if we could spot her.

'We'll meet back here in ten minutes and if you find her, don't let her out of your sight,' he said.

Me and Jit went to the car park first. It was packed with cars and coaches but we couldn't see her anywhere. We walked all the way round, approaching any old Indian woman we could see, and there were quite a few on a coach trip from Birmingham. It was just about to leave and we asked the driver if he had seen her. He shook his head and told us that he had counted his party back onto the coach.

'All here, innit,' he told us. 'Ain't got no extras.'

After asking the driver we went back inside, and I searched the ladies whilst Jit looked in the shops. She wasn't anywhere to be seen. By the time we met up with my parents, my dad looked really worried.

'Where could she have gone?' he asked for about the fourth time.

In the end, after she'd been gone for over twenty minutes, we told the duty manager, who put an announcement over the tannoy system.

'*Would anyone who sees an old Asian lady looking lost please contact the nearest member of staff. She's wearing a traditional Asian outfit and has white hair. Five foot two with a limp and glasses.*'

We were standing right next to the customer service desk when the manager made his announcement and I was well embarrassed. People were looking at us and pointing and stuff.

'I wish I was in the car,' I mumbled to Jit.

'Me too,' he whispered.

'She's always doing this,' moaned my dad. 'Senile old bat.'

'Oh leave her alone, Randeep,' snapped my mum. 'She can't help it . . .'

'Bloody can,' mumbled my dad. 'Does it on purpose.'

We stood and waited for another ten minutes and then the coach driver who we'd spoken to earlier turned up at the desk. My dad saw that he was Sikh and spoke to him in Punjabi, asking if he'd seen Gran.

The coach driver smiled before he answered in his strong Anglo-Indian accent.

'The kids ask me earlier, innit. Said I didn't see her. But when I get back on motorway, one of the women in my party say she at back of coach, drinking tea and eating chapatti with other womens . . .'

My dad groaned.

'She very funny woman,' said the driver.

'Where is she?' asked my mum, in English.

'On the coach. Won't get off. Says that you don't feed her.'

'Oh my God!' I groaned. 'This is just too much!'

My dad shrugged.

'Best go get her then,' he said, thanking the driver, as he led us out to the coach. My mum thanked the duty manager, who was trying really hard not to burst into laughter.

When we got to the coach my gran was sitting at the back, and my dad had to go on and coax her out. The other women, who my gran had been telling lies to, called my dad shameless and evil. As he helped Gran down the steps of the coach, I heard one of the old women shout out, 'She wiped your backside for you and look what you do to her. No shame, you donkey!'

My gran started swearing at him too, and by the time he'd got her back into the car, he was sweating.

'Look at it this way,' my mum told him, smiling: 'things can't get any worse.'

My dad looked at my gran and then at Jit and me. 'Not for me they can't,' he said mysteriously.

I shook my head. 'If you think you're going to lumber Jit and me with her . . .'

'We'll see,' he replied, chuckling to himself.

'Ooloo ka puttha!' spat my gran, which means 'You piece of owl poo.'

I smiled at Jit and shrugged, hoping he wouldn't hold my nutty family against me.

He just picked up his book and started reading.

# SEVENTEEN

We arrived about an hour later and my dad found a place to park the car. Jit was really excited, asking me how close we were to the sea.

'Dunno,' I said.

My dad turned round and smiled at him.

'See those shops?' he asked.

'Yeah?'

'Just the other side of those . . .'

'Wicked!'

'Where are we meeting the rest of the family?' I asked.

'Dunno – Mandeep was supposed to call me when he got here. I'll wait until I hear from him.'

He shot my mum a look and I guessed what it meant. We'd look like an army of Asians invading the beach.

We walked off towards the shops, down a little

lane towards a precinct full of small boutiques and gift shops.

My dad showed the way, telling us that he'd been here loads as a teenager.

'Used to be a good market here. My uncle had a stall.'

The precinct led into a shopping centre, where the shops were exactly the same as every other shopping centre in the country. My mum told my dad that she was tired.

'Can we sit down and get a coffee or something?'

'What?' shouted my gran, so loud that people stopped and looked at us.

'Tea?' my dad shouted at her.

'YES!' she said in an even louder voice.

I looked at Jit and then my mum. 'We're going for a walk,' I told her.

'OK, but don't get lost,' she replied.

My dad snorted. 'You can't get lost around here – it's not big enough.'

'Well just be careful,' added my mum.

'We're going to have lunch at a little place called Chathams,' said my dad. 'There's no point sitting in the car and eating the sandwiches. It'll be horrible.

Besides, they'll keep. Meet us at Chathams in an hour. You can't miss it . . . it's down along the seafront.'

'OK,' I replied, eager to get away.

Jit shrugged and told me that he wanted to go and see the sea. I looked at him like he was mad.

'The *sea*? Have you seen how *cold* it is out there?'

'But that's why I came,' he replied. 'I've never seen it.'

What I really wanted to do was hide somewhere warm, far away from my mad gran, but then I realized that Jit would be really disappointed if he didn't get to go to the seafront. In the end I zipped up my jacket and nodded.

'OK then – but if I catch something, I'm going to beat you up!'

'Yeah, yeah,' grinned Jit. 'It's only a bit of rain, anyway.'

He marched down towards the exit and out into the rain. I waited a moment and then followed him. Outside, it was windy and grey, and as we made our way down to the front, people walking in the opposite direction gave us funny looks.

'They think we're mad,' I pointed out to Jit.

'So? Who cares what they think?' he replied. He

said something else too but his words got lost in a sudden gust of wind.

'Great!' I said.

We passed a few banks and some food places and then rounded a corner. In front of us, across a road, was the beach and then the sea. Jit looked at me, grinned like a little child, and ran across. I waited until the road was clear and followed him. By the time I'd crossed, he was on the sand, heading towards the sea.

'JIT!' I shouted at him, but he didn't hear me. He stood where he was and watched the waves crashing against the shore.

I looked up and down the beach and saw that it was almost deserted. There was a young woman walking a dog, and an Asian man with a blonde woman standing under a shelter, talking. I walked carefully towards Jit and stood next to him.

'It's great, isn't it?' I said to him.

'Yeah,' he replied, lost in the view.

'You really haven't seen the sea before?'

'Nope.'

I put my hand on his shoulder and for once he didn't flinch or look away. Instead he looked at me and smiled.

'Have you ever swum in the sea?' he asked me.

'Yeah – lots!'

'What's it like?'

'Salty, wet, cold if it's around this country.'

'Oh . . .'

'Full of seaweed too.'

'You know people eat that, don't you?' he said.

'What, seaweed?'

He nodded as the young woman ran past us, chasing after her dog.

'Yeah, I saw it on some cookery show on the telly.'

'You're not as stupid as you pretend, are you?' I said, punching him on the arm.

'What do you want to do now?' he asked.

'I thought you wanted to look at the sea?'

'Done it,' he said, matter-of-factly. 'Besides, it's not going anywhere, you get me?'

'I saw a gift shop, back in the little streets by the shopping centre. Maybe we can find your mum a present there?' I suggested.

'Yeah . . . let's do that.'

We walked back up the road, past the shelter where the Asian man and his girlfriend were still sitting, talking to each other. The woman smiled as we passed and

I smiled back. Then I looked at the man and thought that I recognized him. When we'd walked on about twenty metres, I told Jit.

'I've seen that guy somewhere before,' I told him.

'What guy?'

'The Asian bloke back there.'

'Nah – he could be anyone.'

I shook my head.

'No – I've definitely seen his face – just can't remember where, that's all. It'll come to me.'

'Where's this shop then?' he asked, ignoring me.

'Down here,' I said, heading into a side street.

We didn't see anything that Jit wanted in the shop so instead we walked around some more, past amusement arcades and souvenir shops, half of them closed. I suppose it was quite late in the year for tourists. Not that I wanted the Union Jack bowler hats and flags, or the topless postcards. Not to mention candy rock that would break the teeth on a shark and the nasty key rings. We also walked past the entrance to a cave tour, which was still open. The man at the entrance asked if we wanted to come in. I shook my head and said that we would come back after lunch.

'Fair enough,' he said, smiling broadly. 'Bring us a sandwich when you do!'

I looked at the time and told Jit that we needed to find Chathams.

'It's back along the road, I think,' I said.

'Back the way we came?' he asked.

'Yeah.'

'It's quite a small place, ain't it?'

'Very, although there's a load of roads past the seafront and the shops. And that big hill over there.'

Jit looked up and saw what I was on about.

'Is that a castle at the top?' he asked.

'What's left of it.'

'Castles, smugglers' caves – it's great round here. We ain't got none of them things where we live,' he said.

'Yeah, but we've got more people, better shops and lots of other stuff,' I pointed out. 'And besides, it reminds me of them books I used to read when I was a kid . . . *The Famous* something or other.'

Jit grinned. 'I used to read them too – they were lame.'

'Bet they were set in a place like this,' I said.

'Prob'ly,' he said, as we walked back past the shelter where the man I'd recognized had been sitting with his girlfriend. But they were gone so I didn't get another chance to look at him.

'He's gone,' I said out loud, without meaning too.

'Who?' asked Jit.

'That bloke . . . the one I recognized,' I replied.

I didn't have long to wait to see him again. He was with his girlfriend, sitting in the window of Chathams, when we walked in. I smiled at him and he kind of smiled back; I was still wondering how I knew him. Then I saw my dad towards the back of the bar, where the room seemed to lead into another series of caves.

'They're in the back,' I said to Jit. 'Come on.'

I took one more look at the man but he didn't see me this time. He was too busy talking to his girlfriend.

My gran was her usual mad self whilst we were eating. First she took out her false teeth and put them down on the table next to her. Then, when the waitress came to take our orders, she started talking to her in Punjabi. The waitress was really polite and patient, even though she didn't have a clue what my gran was on about. She just smiled and said 'Oh, that's nice' when my gran finished speaking to her. My dad shrugged apologetically at the girl.

'Sorry about that,' he said to her.

'It's no problem,' said the waitress. 'Now what can I get for you?'

When the food arrived, my gran dipped her finger in my mum's glass of water and started cleaning her false teeth.

'*Mum!*' said my dad in Punjabi, only to get a mouthful of abuse.

Jit stared at his food and tried not to crack up with laughter.

'So, Jit,' said my dad. 'Tell me what your old man does again?'

'Huh?' asked Jit, looking up from his plate of fish and chips.

'Your dad – what does he do?'

I shot my dad a glare.

'He's already told you a million times,' I lied.

'I've forgotten,' replied my dad.

'He owns a load of fried chicken takeaways,' said Jit, remembering what he'd said last time.

The truth was that Jit didn't know what his dad did. He hadn't seen him since his parents had split up.

'Oh – only I don't know anyone with your family name who's got fried chicken shops in our city.'

'They're all in Birmingham and Coventry,' lied Jit.

I started feeling really bad for making him tell lies, especially as I was planning to tell my parents the truth anyway. So I jumped in.

'What does it matter what his dad does?' I asked. 'It's not a big deal.'

'I was only asking,' said my dad.

'Does that stupid skinny rat eat anything?' asked my gran in Punjabi.

Jit snorted with the strain of not laughing.

'I'm sorry, Jit,' said my mum. 'For my husband *and* my mother-in-law.'

'It's OK,' said Jit. 'I don't really like talking about my family. I prefer to listen to other people.'

'I see,' replied my mum, looking at my dad.

'So, does our daughter bully you?' asked my dad.

'Dad!'

'Well, you are a bit of a madam,' he told me.

'I don't believe this,' I said.

Jit shrugged. 'She's a bit bossy at school and that,' he replied. 'And she loves to beat us at sprinting and other sports.'

'She doesn't make you do things against your will? Because she used to do that with one of her cousins –

she even made him dress up in a skirt once,' continued my dad.

'I remember that,' said my mum. 'That was Rohan, wasn't it – poor lad.'

'He still hasn't got over it,' added my dad.

Jit looked at me and shook his head. 'No, she doesn't make me do stuff like that,' he said.

My dad nodded.

'Interesting,' he said, 'only I've heard differently.'

The waitress came back before I could ask my dad what he was on about. 'Your friends have arrived,' she told my parents.

My dad looked over my shoulder to the front of the bar and grinned.

Assuming it was my uncle, I didn't bother turning round. It was Jit who saw them first.

'Oh crap!' he said.

'What's wrong?' I asked, before turning round and finding out for myself.

'Hi, Suky,' said Imtiaz, half smiling.

My mouth fell open and my heart sank. I gulped down air. Behind Imi were his parents, smiling at me.

# EIGHTEEN

'Imtiaz told us everything,' said my dad, after I'd recovered from my shock.

'I tried to warn you,' Imi said to me. 'But you didn't return my call.'

I shot my mum a look.

'Don't look at *me* like that,' she said. 'I'm not the one who's been lying, am I?'

'But you let me and Jit carry on all day today and you knew,' I said.

My dad chuckled. So did Imi's.

'We wanted to see what else you'd come up with,' he told me.

'I can't believe that you kept it up for so long,' said Imi's mum.

'Shows a great deal of initiative,' said Mr Dhondy.

'And slyness,' added my dad.

'I'm so sorry,' I said, beginning to cry.

Jit just sat where he was, looking at anything but

the people sitting around him. The waitress had moved us to a bigger table and we were the only people left in there. Even the owners were listening in on my shame. I looked at Jit and told *him* I was sorry too.

'Poor lad,' said my dad. 'You made him tell lies just so you could hide the truth.'

Jit looked up at the mention of his name. 'It wasn't all Suky's fault,' he replied. 'I went along with it and I didn't have to.'

My mum smiled at him. 'Yes, we know that. But that just makes you a good friend, as far as I'm concerned. Devious, but a good friend.'

'And I didn't help either,' said Imi. 'I let Suky and Jit take all the risks and didn't do a thing. I could have told my parents.'

'Well you did eventually,' pointed out his mum.

'Yeah – only after those two idiots came round and grassed us all up!' he said.

What had happened was this. Justin and Andy had carried out their threat to tell the parents, only they had told Imi's parents and not mine. That had been on the Wednesday afternoon, after Andy had overheard Hannah and Grace talking. As we were all rushing to my house, thinking that Justin and Andy had gone

there, the bullies were actually at Imi's house. Not that
his mum had been too happy to see them.

'Very strange young men,' she told me. 'Sneering,
ugly boys, and one of them had the most unfortunate
hair.'

Imi's parents didn't confront him because they
wanted to speak to my parents first, and besides,
they didn't know that Justin and Andy weren't just
causing mischief. So Mrs Dhondy called my mum,
who just happened to be sitting reading the phone bill
at the time, and she checked the numbers I'd dialled
the most. Between them, they worked out that I had
actually been on the phone to Imi and not Jit, as I'd
claimed. Then, between them and our fathers, they'd
come up with a devious little plan of their own. Which
I was finding it hard to understand.

'But why all the trouble to bring us down *here* and
tell us?' I asked. 'And lying about Uncle Mandeep
coming too?'

My dad grinned at Imi's dad.

'You kids aren't the only ones who can play games,'
said Mr Dhondy.

'We thought we'd give you a little taste of your own
medicine,' added my dad. 'Not nice, is it?'

He was right. I looked at Imi and tried to smile but it came out all wrong. Imi shrugged. He'd found out what was going on yesterday evening, which was why he'd called frantically. Not the stuff about the trip, but the fact that his parents knew about me. He'd found his own phone bill, with my number underlined in red pen and my name written next to it. But when he'd called, my mum had been first to the phone and the same thing had happened when I'd called back.

'So Imi was actually *in* when I rang back?' I asked his mum.

'Yes, sweetheart, but I couldn't let you go and spoil our fun by talking to him, could I?' she said, shaking her head to make the point.

'And you were all in on it?'

This time my dad started laughing really hard. When I asked what was happening he said something really weird. He said 'Michael, too'. I looked at my mum.

'As in Michael *Parkhurst*? Grace's father?'

'Oh my God – did he know too?'

My dad held his sides and pointed to the door. I turned to see a smiling Mr Parkhurst with Grace, Dean and Hannah.

'Oh *great*! Bring the whole bloody school, why don't you?' I snapped.

'Oh don't be so silly, Suky. It could have been much worse. Besides, your friends only found out on Friday night so they didn't get the chance to tell you.'

'On pain of a terrible and lingering death,' said Mr Parkhurst.

The adults said their hellos, except for my gran, who just sat looking out of the window. Grace, Dean and Hannah were all wearing really long faces.

'Are you OK?' asked Grace.

'Yeah – why wouldn't I be? Sitting here with my shame exposed to the entire world . . . I'm peachy.'

'I was only asking,' she replied. 'How about you, Jit?'

'I'm all right,' he told her. 'Feel a bit bad though – because of all the lies and that.'

'Don't worry about that,' interrupted my dad. 'That was Suky's fault, not yours, and besides, I like you, whether you're going out with her or not. I was hoping we could still be friends?'

Jit looked at me and I nodded. 'I'd like that,' he told my dad.

'Well then,' said Grace's father. 'I guess we should all have a drink and chill out.'

'Dad!' said Grace.

'Yeah, Mr P,' teased Dean. 'Time we "chilled out",
you get me?'

'I certainly do, bro,' winked Mr Parkhurst.

Hannah and Grace looked at each other and started
giggling. I went over to Jit.

'I'm really sorry,' I said to him.

'Me too,' he replied.

'What have you got to be sorry for?'

'I could have just said no,' he pointed out.

I shook my head.

'No – this is down to me and Imi. No one else.'

'She's right,' added Imi. 'You've been a really good
friend and I shouldn't have acted up over it, so I'm
sorry too.'

Imi's mum coughed. 'Well if the apologies are going
round then I suggest that you offer one to the rest of
us too,' she said.

I looked at Imi, grinned and then shrugged.

We spent the rest of the day doing our own thing. Jit
and the others went exploring, whilst the parents just
moved from café to bar to café again. I took Imi down
to the beach and we sat in the shelter that I'd seen

earlier. But not before we'd both been taken to one side by our parents.

'What else did your parents say to you?' he asked me.

'Nothing really – they were so cool about it.'

'Mine too,' he admitted.

'So basically we were worried about nothing at all?' I asked.

'Looks that way. I can't believe that they didn't get really angry though.'

I shrugged. 'Maybe they will when we get home?' I suggested.

'I can't see it,' said Imi. 'You heard the way they are with each other. My mum loves your mum.'

'Yeah, and our dads are as stupid and silly and childish as each other,' I added.

'Exactly,' replied Imi.

I thought about what that meant – the fact that we wouldn't have to go around hiding any more – and I smiled.

'You nuts or something?' asked Imi.

'*What?*'

'You're just staring out into the sea, smiling at nothing,' he said.

'I'm just thinking about school and not having to hide our relationship from anyone.'

'Yeah – that'll be a lot less stressful,' he admitted.

I turned to him and gave him a kiss: you know, a quiet moment, on our own? Fat chance. Somebody wolf-whistled and then cheered. I looked up and saw my friends, grinning back at me.

'Stop that this instant!' demanded Grace.

'Yeah,' said Dean. 'Come and check out the sights!'

'I wanna go in the caves,' said Hannah.

'Me too,' added Jit.

I looked at Imi and smiled. 'Oh come on then!' I said, standing up and joining my friends.

As we walked towards the smugglers' caves, Jit pointed something out to the rest of us. 'We've still got a problem with Justin and Andy,' he said.

'Oh yeah,' agreed Grace.

'Don't worry about that,' Dean said to us all proudly.

'Why?' I asked. 'Have you come up with something?'

'Nah,' he replied. 'But I will. Them two bwoi can wait a while.'

'Yeah, I suppose they can,' I said to him.

'Still be there on Monday,' added Hannah.

The wind started to get up again and the rain clouds opened.

'Some day to come to the seaside,' moaned Grace. 'I mean, none of the *locals* are even outdoors, never mind walking along the coastal road. They're probably all watching us from their windows thinking, *Look at those mental city folk*. And I'm not mental – I'm *not*!'

'Grace?' I said.

'Yes, sweetie?' she asked, smiling.

'Will you shut up?'

'OK then . . .'

I grinned at Jit for what felt like the hundredth time.

'No more jugglin' then?' he said to me.

'I suppose not,' I replied. 'And I was having such fun too!'

I worked out who the Asian guy was as well. He was *only* the *author* of the book that I'd given to Jit. Talk about coincidences. *Real* luck would have consisted of me recognizing who he was straight away, and having my book at hand. But then again, considering how easily I had got away with my deception, and the way my parents had reacted, I guess I'd used up my luck quota for, like, the millenium or something. Oh well . . .

# Two more tales from Devana High

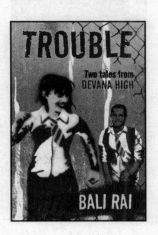

**GRACE** and her mates hate late lunches and being last in the canteen queue. They always get stuck with the rank leftovers. But then they think of a wicked plan . . .

**DEAN** is always up for making some extra cash. When he gets his hands on a sweet stash of mobile phones and games, he knows he's going to make millions. Unless school bully Jason makes trouble instead . . .

# For older readers
## (Un)arranged Marriage

bali rai

(un)arranged marriage

'*Harry and Ranjit were waiting for me – waiting to take me to Derby, to a wedding. My wedding. A wedding that I hadn't asked for, that I didn't want. To a girl I didn't know . . .*

*If they had bothered to open their eyes, they would have seen me: seventeen, angry, upset but determined – determined to do my own thing, to choose my own path in life . . .*'

**Set partly in the UK and partly in the Punjab region of India, this is a fresh, bitingly perceptive look at one young man's fight to free himself from family expectations and to be himself, free to dance to his own tune.**

# For older readers
## Rani & Sukh

*'Man, she's wicked, like one of them
Bollywood actresses . . .'*

Sukh reckons Rani is the most fanciable girl in
school. She's got just the kind of look
he goes for . . .

Rani can't stop thinking about Sukh either. Talk
about fit. Beautiful amber-brown eyes, like pools
you could jump into . . .

But Rani is a Sandhu, and Sukh is a Bains – and
sometimes names can lead to terrible trouble . . .

**A powerful and gripping novel that sweeps the reader from
modern-day Britain to the Punjab in the 1960s and back again in
a ceaseless cycle of tragedy and conflict.**

# For older readers
## The Crew

*'Mess with one of us – then you have to deal with all of us . . .'*

Positive attitudes only. That's the Crew: Billy, Jas, Della, Will and Ellie. And where they live – in the concrete heart of a big city – you need a crew to back you up.

Then one day they find a fortune in notes and life suddenly becomes very dangerous . . .

**A no-holds-barred thriller set against the gritty reality of life many British kids must face on a day-to-day basis.**

# For older readers
## The Whisper

As tough and uncompromising
as the city streets it depicts

bali rai
the whisper

The Crew didn't think things could ever get that bad again. They were dead wrong.

Whatever you know, whatever you see, you keep your mouth shut – it's one of the first rules of the ghetto. But now the rule's been broken.

Someone's grassing up the dealers and the whisper on the street says it's Nanny and the Crew.

They need to act fast to salvage their rep before the situation explodes . . .

# For older readers
## The Last Taboo

*'Tyrone leaned across the table and gave me a long kiss. When I eventually opened my eyes I saw an Asian couple, middle-aged, on the next table along. You know that phrase — if looks could kill? Well, I was dead.'*

Simran falls for Tyrone from the moment she spots him in the crowd. He's gorgeous and won't take no for an answer. There's just one problem — Tyrone is black and Simran's not sure how her family will react.

When two of Simran's cousins from the Asian gang the Desi Posse find out that she is seeing Tyrone, things start to get out of control . . .